TH
HARARE
SYNDROME

Kennedy Mupomba

MAPLE
PUBLISHERS

The Harare Syndrome

Author: Kennedy Mupomba

Copyright © Kennedy Mupomba (2022)

First Published in 2022

ISBN 978-1-915492-20-3 (Paperback)
          978-1-915492-21-0 (Ebook)

Book cover design and Book layout by:
          White Magic Studios
          www.whitemagicstudios.co.uk

Published by:
          Maple Publishers
          1 Brunel Way,
          Slough,
          SL1 1FQ, UK
          www.maplepublishers.com

A CIP catalogue record for this title is available from the British Library.

Author's Email: kmupomba@yahoo.co.uk

Characters

Court officials

Magistrate

Prosecutor

Court Orderly

Interpreter

Jabu [*magistrate*]

Mr Ndebvu [*Busani's lawyer*]

Joe [*interpreter*]

Prison Officers [*two*]

Bank staff

Busani [*bank teller*]

Tom [*bank teller*]

Nomsa [*bank teller*]

Ashton [*bank security officer*]

Jimmy [*bank teller*]

John Mapurisa [*chief bank security officer*]

Dehwa [*bank executive*]

Other characters

Mrs Bunda [*Busani's mother*]

Mrs Moyo [*Jimmy's mother*]

Mrs Rengwe [*interpreter's mother-in-law*]

Police Spokeswoman

Members of the Gallery

Martha [*magistrate's wife*]

Police Sergeant

Rovapasi Zvaramba [*television presenter*]

Vengai [*Busani's brother*]

Mr Rengwe [*Interpreter's father-in-law*]

Rose [*interpreter's wife*]

Accused Person

Investigating Officer [*I.O*]

Departure Help Desk Attendant

Police Constable

CONTENTS

ACT I

Scene I

Takes place at a trendy city bar, where Jimmy is seated in-between Tom and Nomsa. They are having exotic drinks and engaged in a conversation.

Jimmy: [*looking haggard*]: I am at a loss with the arrest of Busani. I have had a sleepless night.

Nomsa: [*touching Jimmy's hand*]: Jimmy, we are also very worried with this development.

Tom: I am equally alarmed by the turn of events.

Jimmy: She has been in the police cells for forty-eight hours now. Upon visiting her, I noted that she is a total wreck in those filthy Harare Central Police Station cells.

Nomsa: One can starve to death in there. Can you imagine, the police said those with alternative means must encourage their friends and relatives to bring them food.

Tom: Is it not their duty to feed those whom they arrest?

Jimmy: That was way back then. When I went to see Busani, she asked me to bring her food from Nando's and a fat police officer at the station demanded that I should also bring him food from Nando's.

Nomsa: No wonder many of them are fat in contrast with the starving majority.

Tom: I could not stand the stench in those overcrowded cells.

Jimmy: I was horrified to note that instead of a proper modern toilet, there is an overflowing bucket used as a toilet in the corner of the holding cell where my lovely Busani was.

Tom: Well, I understand those police cells are hotels in comparison with the remand prison and worse still, the supposed toilets at Chikurubi Maximum Security Prison.

Nomsa: You can say that again. A few weeks ago, there was a serious riot led by some infamous prison inmates.

Jimmy: [*imploringly*]: Please don't talk about that place. I do not even want to think of that dungeon. Can we instead talk of getting her out, please?

Tom: Of course, Jimmy, that is why we are gathered here though I was expecting more bank tellers to turn up.

Nomsa: Guys, ever since the arrest of Busani, our colleagues are in panic mode. The media has not helped either by suggesting that millions could have been siphoned.

Jimmy: It is John who is feeding the media with falsehoods. While the taking of money occurred, I am doubtful that the figure runs into millions of US dollars.

Tom: I am not surprised though; it could be more. Look at what most of us have done with the money, ranging from buying properties, flashy cars and going on exotic holidays.

Nomsa: I think Tom you are right, some of us became very careless, flaunting our wealth.

Jimmy: [*rubbing his hands*]: Sometimes, I think of throttling Vengai to death.

Tom: [*playfully pats Jimmy's back*]. You have yourself a fine future brother in-law there!

Nomsa: Busani has helped several times that useless brother of hers. Vengai comes with business schemes that never come to fruition.

Jimmy: I have spoken to Busani about it, but she has been adamant that she has to help her kin. However, we all know that once he gets the money, he rushes to the trendiest bars. He will then in a drunken stupor, penniless, stagger back to Busani, armed with a new, foolish business proposal and she gives him money again.

Tom: Never mind Vengai. Let us to talk about this grave matter that is staring at us.

Jimmy: I have paid the best lawyer in town, the greatly revered Mr Ndebvu.

Tom: Good choice, he is a celebrated lawyer.

Nomsa: Are we banking only on a lawyer to spring Busani out of prison guys?

Jimmy: Vengai also said court officials could be approached to facilitate her release.

Tom: That would be double re-assurance if that can be arranged.

Jimmy: He says his friends in the legal fraternity advised him to seek court officials.

Nomsa: So that is either the prosecutor or the magistrate?

Tom: He said the way it works is that the prosecutor can oppose bail, but the magistrate can overrule the prosecutor. So, the magistrate has the ultimate say in the matter.

Jimmy: Well, given that John has been bragging that he is on friendly terms with all prosecutors at all courts; Busani's chance will definitely be with the magistrate.

Tom: On another note, guys, we need to think about our own freedoms. Do you think John will look the other way given the little money we have given him?

Nomsa: There has been panic among bank tellers since Busani's arrest. I understand John has clandestinely received substantial monies from bank tellers for him not to look into their fraudulent banking practices.

Jimmy: Hopefully, the money we have given him will dissuade him from looking into our nefarious activities.

Nomsa: I don't think we have heard the last of him.

Tom: You are spot-on Nomsa. He is a sly one. Even though he has not directly asked for a bribe to look the other way, by suggesting that prosecutors are his mates, he is in a way saying, pay up or else.

Jimmy: Yes, he is a furtive one. He will be back for more.

Nomsa: So, what can we do?

Tom: My friends, events in the next few days will enable us to make informed decisions.

Nomsa: Maybe, it is time to make friends with the wind.

Jimmy: I can't go anyway without Busani. I love her so much.

Tom: [*laughs*]: Jimmy, whereas they say till death do us part, it may come to imprisonment do us part on your part and Busani soon.

Nomsa: [*chidingly*]: Be nice to Jimmy now, Tom.

Tom: Sorry, Jimmy.

Jimmy: Let us wait for tomorrow.

Nomsa: There is always light at the end of the tunnel guys.

Tom: I have a terrible premonition about tomorrow.

[Exit all].

Enter John and a barman

John: [*soliloquising at a trendy city hotel bar*]: Life is strange, that I, [*rubs his hands gleefully*] John Mapurisa, once a poor civil servant, eking a living out of corruption, now find myself catapulted into the banking sector, a land of milk and honey [*he licks his lips*). I now live far from the madding crowd, in the leafy suburbs, far away from the ghetto. I now drive a brand new four by four truck, all courtesy of the bank [*he points a finger in the air*], my God is up there. A thick blanket of fear has enveloped the bank and the bank tellers are running amok since Busani's arrest.

In helping the police in investigating the fraudulent activities, I have suddenly become the man of the moment at the bank. They know that if I merely point a finger at any of them, the investigating officer will swoop upon them. Now the fraudsters jostle to line my pockets with not bond notes, but proper US dollars. I think there is plenty more dollars hidden away. So, what is needed here is for me to up the ante [*by a hand gesture, he summons the barman to come to him*]. Same please, barman and keep the change [*he pushes a ward of US dollars to the barman*].

Barman: No problem, Sir [*he moves off soliloquising*]. Harare city, this city of Harare is full of mysteries. This former detective used to sponge off criminals in this very bar. Ever since he moved to work at the bank, he became capable of paying for his own lagers.

However, since yesterday, he drinks and eats the executive stuff only and with reckless disregard. He lives the lifestyle of artisanal gold miners, the so-called *Makorokoza*. May his streak of luck continue for long. I call upon his ancestors and God to doubly protect him from harm as his tips are very welcome.

Enter the prosecutor

John: [*hails the prosecutor*]: My friend, that was very fast!

Prosecutor: [*they shake hands*]: If you are a civil servant in Harare and someone calls you mid-month to come to a hotel, you don't walk, you run, my friend!

John: [*laughs*]: You can say that again. Times are tight for civil servants in this city. Remember, I also experienced droughts of money before I joined the bank.

Prosecutor: [*sits next to John at the bar*]. Our salaries hardly cover our daily needs. Inflation has eroded our meagre earnings. Many civil servants have ditched the luxury of boarding public transport and now trudge many kilometres to work. I see many carrying lunch boxes from home.

John: That is terrible.

Prosecutor [*smiles*]: Not all of us are starving though.

John: Yes, those that are enterprising are doing well.

Prosecutor: I don't suppose you called me over for a lecture on theories of poverty [*he beckons the barman come to him*].

John: [*laughs*]: I read somewhere that poverty is one of the five giants that stalks poor people! I have a proposition that will stop this giant stalking you forever, my dear friend.

Prosecutor: [*brightens up*]: Really?

John: Forget your usual beer my friend today; I will buy you upmarket waters.

Prosecutor: [*to the barman*]: Get me the most expensive drink you have in here.

John: [*barman does not move and John sternly talks to him*]. Move my friend, give my very important guest your best: it is all on me!

Barman: Sorry, boss [*he moves off very fast to mix a drink*].

Prosecutor: So, what's up my dear friend?

John: At my workplace, we lost hundreds of thousands or maybe millions of US dollars in fraudulent activities.

Prosecutor: Oh, that is terrible. I suppose the bank is looking up to you to bring the crooks to book.

Barman: [*brings a glassful of liquor and places it before the prosecutor*]: There you are Sir, the best in the house.

Prosecutor: [*he takes a sip, savours it and nods his head*]: Thanks barman, this is really good stuff.

Barman: [*smiles*]: Anytime, Sir [*and he moves away to attend to another customer*].

John: You are right. The bank is livid and wants to recover every penny stolen. I need to impress the bank. That is why I need you, my friend.

Prosecutor: How can help?

John: One bank teller has been arrested so far, and knowing the corrupt practices at the courts, she may regain her freedom clandestinely. I am therefore treading warily. In a bid to stifle any prospects of freedom for her, I have demanded that the investigating officer must hand the matter to the cleanest prosecutor.

Prosecutor: [*looking surprised*]: Who is this angelic prosecutor?

John: [*laughs*]: What I need is a prosecutor who understands the subtleness of Harare. I need an articulate prosecutor, a prosecutor who improvises and can bend the law in the full glare of all and sundry to suit our needs. I am looking no further than you, my good friend. We have previously and successfully collaborated during my time in the police force, you are very good.

Prosecutor: [*wagging a finger at his friend*]: John, John. To engage in corrupt practice is walking on a very slippery surface. Our President of Zimbabwe, popularly called the crocodile is matching that animal's characteristics by eating up corrupt people. Many are now languishing in prisons, his SACU and ZACC are working twenty-four seven, sniffing out corrupt people and fervently taking or seeking to take their ill-gotten properties. I hung my boots a few days ago after a close shave with the law long arm of the law, my friend. I am done.

John: [*imploringly*]: Listen, my friend. There is no danger at all for you in this good enterprise. It is the tricksters whose liberties are at stake. In fact, it is your name that will be sung for ages.

Prosecutor: So, what do I have I to do?

John: It is simple. You eat what I bring you and not what the accused person's relatives or friends offer you.

Prosecutor: Are you saying I should not be bribed?

John: Yes. I have insisted that the matter be brought to your good office.

Prosecutor: If the police are opposing bail and for good reasons, I will oppose the granting of bail in court without fear or favour. That is my job.

John: You don't understand fully my friend. From my preliminary investigations, millions were siphoned from the bank and the money is out there and can be used to influence even you. The vultures, as we speak, are circling. We need this woman to be residing at the remand prison while we finalise investigations.

Prosecutor: Yes, it is a common trend in the city for accused persons to seek to bribe the prosecutor or the magistrate or both.

John: If you do as I say, you are in for a lot of money which you never imagined owning in your lifetime.

Prosecutor: [*laughs*): I don't suppose you mean the bank is going to give me money to oppose bail.

John: [*laughs*]: Banks are not that generous! As I said, a number of bank tellers were involved, and it is from them that I will extract your fat fee.

Prosecutor: How will you do that?

John: Have you forgotten so soon that I was a chief inspector at CID Fraud Squad. That squad comprise of the best brains in the police force and banks are very eager to have them as in-house security staff as we are thorough in what we do. I can manipulate the course of events and already, I have set the wheels in motion.

Prosecutor: [*raises his hand to the barman who in turn mixes him another drink*]: What have you done?

John: [*he takes from his jacket pocket two bundles of US dollars and passes them over to the prosecutor*]: There is more from where that came from.

Prosecutor: [*whistles as he pockets the money*]. This is serious money, my friend. Whatever you suggest, I am your man.

John: That is a mere fraction, Mr Prosecutor. We are coming to your office with the investigating officer tomorrow and the accused person. For obvious reasons, the investigating officer will not be privy to our dealings.

Prosecutor: Of course, the less people involved, the bulkier will our purses be.

John: Quite right, my friend. I have to go and see the investigating officer now, but enjoy the drinks [*he pulls a ward of US dollars and puts them into the prosecutor's hand*].

Prosecutor: [*sounding surprised*]: But John, you have given me enough already. I am not that greedy.

John [*smiles*]: It is not my money, my friend. Enjoy it [*and exits*].

Prosecutor [*soliloquises*]. In all my dealings, I have never had such easy pickings [*he looks at the bundles of US dollars*]. With this being my last corrupt enterprise, this amounts to going out with a bang [*the barman brings him his drink*].

Barman: Your drink, Sir.

Prosecutor: [*handing him a US$100 note*]: It is a beautiful day, therefore, have a drink on me, but make sure my glass is ever full till you close this place down tonight.

Barman: [*smiles*]: Always at your service, Sir.

[Exit both].

Scene II

Opens with the Investigating Officer (I.O), John and Busani entering the prosecutor's office at the Harare Magistrates Court. Busani is in handcuffs.

Prosecutor: [*to his visitors*]: Good morning, gentlemen [*he ignores Busani*].

I.O: Good morning, Mr Prosecutor.

John: [*shaking the prosecutor's hand*]. Good morning, Sir.

Busani: Good morning, Sir [*the prosecutor does not even look at her*].

Prosecutor: What brings you to my office?

I.O: I came specifically to your office after the bank being represented by Mr John Mapurisa who is here with me indicated that you are, in his professional experience, the best prosecutor to handle this case.

John: This case Mr Prosecutor involves a lot of money and most of it is still to be recovered. My bank is very worried, its stocks have fallen since this matter emerged.

Given the corrupt practices that have become the order of the day at these courts; the bank has tasked me with seeing to it that this matter is handled by untainted hands. From my previous investigations as a member of CID, it is in my professional opinion, that we can get justice through you prosecuting this matter, Sir.

Prosecutor: You need not worry, Sir, prosecuting without fear or favour is our business [*to the I.O*]: Let me see what you have officer.

I.O: [*hands papers to the prosecutor*]: Mr Prosecutor, what John is saying is true; her relatives [*pointing at Busani*] are at this very court and will try everything to cause her release.

Prosecutor: [*reads the papers*]: So, you are opposed to the granting of bail, officer?

I.O: Very strongly, Sir. If she is released, she will interfere with investigations which are still in their infancy. She is also a risk flight as the matter involves hundreds of thousands of US dollars.

Busani: [*pleadingly*]: Please, please, Sir, I won't interfere with your investigations. I will not run away. My father passed away and it is only me who is looking after my terminally ill old mother.

I.O: Mr Prosecutor, her brother can look after their mother very well in her absence. All he has to do is to stop buying everyone a drink in posh clubs.

Prosecutor: [*to Busani*]: Sorry madam, we can't do that. I agree with the investigating officer.

I.O: She is being represented by Mr Ndebvu. I told him that we will bringing the matter to your office.

Prosecutor: Yes, the gentleman rung me expressing his interest in this matter. He said he is on his way and knowing him, he will try every trick in the book to get her out of prison.

Busani: [*pleadingly*]: Please, please, Sir, don't be hush with me. I didn't do all those things the police are alleging. I am innocent, please, Sir.

Prosecutor: [*ignores her pleas and addresses the I.O*]: Officer, take her to the holding cells and instruct the clerk of court to open a court record for the matter. Tell her relatives and other interested parties that the matter will be heard in my court, that is court number seventeen.

I.O: Thank you Mr Prosecutor for your great insight. This case has attracted unprecedented interest. Journalists have been jostling to take pictures of her as we came in [*exits with a sobbing Busani*].

Prosecutor: [*turns to John and smiles*]: With the money you gave me yesterday, I made up for time lost by drinking the best alcohols in town. Who said civil servants should not wine and dine on ill-gotten money?

John: [*rubbing his hands gleefully*]: As I said yesterday, the other bank tellers are squirming [*he whispers*]: If you, successfully oppose bail today, they will see the precariousness of their positions. We will exploit their vulnerability to line our pockets with US dollars, my friend.

Prosecutor: [*smiles*]: You know me very well my friend. I can twist the law to suit our needs.

John: Yes, we have successfully done graver deeds in the past when I was in the police force. But the accused person has armed herself with that Ndebvu, an articulate and eloquent lawyer. I am worried…

Prosecutor: [*cuts him off*]: Don't worry; many highly esteemed lawyers have parted ways with their clients in my court. I will see you after the case.

John: Please don't let me down.

[*Exit all*]

Scene III

Takes place outside the court room where the case is to be heard. Vengai approaches the court interpreter.

Vengai: Excuse me Sir, may I please speak to you for a second?

Interpreter: [*detaches himself from the crowd and follows Vengai*]: Yes, what is it?

Vengai: My sister took some money from her workplace and is appearing in your court today. We urgently need some help.

Interpreter: I am just an interpreter, not the magistrate who decides cases, so how can I be of assistance?

Vengai: The police are opposing bail and I know the prosecutor can override them by not opposing bail in court. We understand, however, that the bank security officer and the prosecutor are friends. The security officer told my sister's workmates that he will use his influence to see to it that my sister rots in prison.

Interpreter: If you know how I can help you, then get to the point quickly as the court is about to sit.

Vengai: [*whispers into the interpreter's ear amidst furtively glancing around*]: Can the magistrate help us by granting her bail? We still have the larger part of the money.

Interpreter: That is an extreme proposition my friend. It is highly illegal. You could end up in prison alongside your sister.

Vengai: [*smiles*]: I know my brother, but this being Harare, we know things can happen.

Interpreter: Why don't you hire a lawyer?

Vengai: We have hired the best around, but between you and me, we know the powerhouse is the magistrate. We want to be sure she gets out and money is not a problem at all. Money is nothing to us, my friend.

Interpreter: Okay, let me see what I can do. I will see you soon.

[*Exit both*].

Scene IV

Opens in the magistrate's office, where the magistrate and the interpreter are having tea.

Magistrate: Anything interesting today in our court, my friend?

Interpreter: [*smiles*]: Yes, Your Worship.

Magistrate: Come now, Mr Interpreter, cut out the Your Worship thing. You know I don't like you addressing me like that in private.

Interpreter: [*smiles*]: Sorry, Your Worship.

Magistrate: [*gleefully rubs his hands*]: By coming to my office, it is indicative of something lucrative being afoot my dear friend.

Interpreter: Yes, and that is if you can pull this one out.

Magistrate: [*smiles*]: By hook or crook, you know by now that nothing stands in His Worship's way.

Interpreter: That is why I am here.

Magistrate: I need money desperately as my landlord is threatening to evict us this weekend. The boarding school also rang me yesterday demanding that I cough up a large sum of money for my children's boarding fees. It is difficult to get money to pay boarding school fees for four children. They are likely be kicked out by the end of this week. Can you imagine the embarrassment?

To make things worse, the garage won't release my car until I pay for the extensive repairs they undertook. Life has become very difficult for me, my friend. There is no light at the end of the tunnel.

Interpreter: Talking of problems, my wife has been pestering me daily. She wants me to buy a house in that upmarket housing scheme. She is deaf to my answers that I do not even have the deposit required.

However, your problems and mine can be wiped off this very day. I have been approached by a man whose sister stole a substantial amount of money from a bank. She is appearing in our court.

The prosecutor, I understand is opposing the granting of bail vehemently and even though they have hired a lawyer to assist her, they want a guarantee that she will be granted bail by Your Worship.

Magistrate: How much do they have?

Interpreter: He said money is not a problem. The larger part of the loot has not been recovered by the dozy police, so it's there for the picking.

Magistrate: [*smiles*]: Well, if she has a lawyer, that will make things easier for me. It's a deal. You know I can't be seen to be talking to accused persons' relatives in public, so I will let you do as per our custom.

Interpreter: [*exiting*]: No problem, I will sort this out as usual.

Magistrate: [*rubbing his hands gleefully, he soliloquises*]: The common assumption that graduating with a law degree will get you rich in no time at all is just a myth. Instead, poverty has stalked me for a long, long time. However, with bankers involved in this matter, this could be the end of my woes. Researchers have theorised that poverty is a circle, my father died a pauper, but I am going to break out of that cycle, come hell or thunder [*exit*].

Scene V

Opens with Mr Ndebvu having a conversation with the prosecutor in the latter's office.

Ndebvu: [*on his feet*]: Good morning, Mr Prosecutor.

Prosecutor: Good morning, Mr Ndebvu.

Ndebvu: I hope it will also be a good morning for my client held at these courts. As I said during our telephone conversation this morning, I am representing Busani Bunda. I take it she is already here.

Prosecutor: That is correct. I have vetted her papers and found that they disclose an offence.

Ndebvu: May I have a look at the state papers such that I can confer with her before the court sits?

Prosecutor: [*he hands the lawyer papers*]: There you go.

Ndebvu: Thank you [*he reads the state papers*].

Prosecutor: If you are ready, we can go into court in the next thirty minutes.

Ndebvu: [*placing the state case papers in his briefcase*]: I don't understand why the state is opposing bail; you don't even have a case at all. The reason that she may take flight are unfounded, Mr Prosecutor.

Prosecutor: The fears are well founded, counsel.

Ndebvu: [*angrily*]: You are not applying your mind to the circumstances of this case [*he bangs the table top with his hand*]: This is rubbish!

Prosecutor: You tell that to the magistrate.

Ndebvu: There is a growing habit by prosecutors of opposing bail for no apparent reason at these rotten courts.

Prosecutor: [*sneers*]: I am not aware of those statistics.

Ndebvu: I think this issue needs to be taken up with the Prosecutor General. The cadre of current prosecutors leaves a lot to be desired.

Prosecutor: [*glares at Mr Ndebvu*]: Meaning?

Ndebvu: During our days as prosecutors, these offices were held in high esteem, Mr Prosecutor. It was all about the application of pure law, not this rubbish.

Prosecutor: [*laughs*]: We practice law at these courts, not village law.

Ndebvu: Not at all, things far removed from the proper administration of justice are happening here.

Prosecutor: [*sternly*]: You can do your posturing in court Mr Ndebvu, not in my office.

Ndebvu: Of course, I will see you in court. I will confer with my client before then [*exit*].

Prosecutor [*soliloquises*]: Those days of lawyers carrying out bulging, worn out briefcases full of irrelevant legal books for the purposes of instilling fear in court officials are over. Arming themselves with heavy loads of legal books is also designed to impress lay persons in the gallery, but not even one book is opened up during the court proceedings.

Well, he will leave these buildings without his client today. I will strike fear in the hearts of those bank thieves still out there. If this accused person lands in prison today, her fellow thieves, currently roaming free, will shower us with money to ward off instant incarceration [*exit*].

ACT II

Scene I

Opens in the court room with the court hearing another case before Busani's case. The gallery is packed with Busani's relatives, friends, workmates, journalists and the general public.

Magistrate: [*to an accused person in the dock*]: You will appear in this court tomorrow morning at nine for your trial. Bring any witnesses you think might extricate you from these very serious charges you are facing. Do you understand?

Accused Person: [*raises his hand*]: I have a request, Your Worship.

Magistrate: Yes?

Accused Person: [*pleadingly*]: My wife is in hospital; may you postpone this matter to next month so that I can be there for her?

Magistrate: [*chuckles*]: Are you a doctor of medicine? [*gallery laughs*].

Accused Person: No, not at all, Your Worship.

Magistrate: So how will you help your wife?

Accused Person: They said at the hospital that she needs moral support. So, I have to be at her bedside.

Magistrate: [*sternly*]: My friend, you must present yourself here tomorrow. If it becomes necessary for the police to arrest you at your wife's hospital bedside, that may worsen her condition. Courts business takes precedent over hospital matters. So be very careful about playing hide and seek with my court [*gallery laughs*].

Court Orderly: [*rises from a desk behind the bar and shouts out*]: Silence in court!

Accused Person: [*bows his head*]: I will be here, Your Worship [*and exits*].

Magistrate: [*to the public prosecutor*]: Any other business, Mr Prosecutor?

Prosecutor: [*stands up and looks towards the court exit door*]: Yes, Your Worship, Mr Ndebvu who is just walking in has a matter before this court [*he sits down*].

Ndebvu: [*stands at the bar*]: Good morning, Your Worship.

Magistrate: Good morning, defence counsel [*Mr Ndebvu sits next to the prosecutor at the bar*]: Mr Prosecutor shall we hear the case then?

Prosecutor: [*stands up*]: May it please the court to hear the matter of the State versus Busani Bunda [*he then addresses a prison officer seated in the dock*]: Officer, may you please bring into the court Busani Bunda.

Prison Officer: Yes, Your Worship [*she disappears into a side room and ushers in Busani whose handcuffs has since been removed into the dock*].

Magistrate: [*turns to Busani*]: May you state your full names to the court please?

Busani: [*looks at the magistrate*]: Busani Bunda, Your Worship.

Ndebvu: [*stands up*]: I represent the accused person in this matter, Your Worship. My client does not need the services of the interpreter. She is able to follow and participate in the proceedings in English.

Magistrate: Thank you defence counsel. Any complaints against the police in the manner they handled your client?

Ndebvu: My client was held in the most squalid conditions at the Harare Central Police Station and these infringed her fundamental human rights. Our superior courts have condemned those police cells many times, Your Worship.

Magistrate: Well, Mr Ndebvu, the whole legal fraternity condemns the grimy police holding cells, but there is nothing much we can do. All we can do is to wait upon the powers that be to correct the anomaly. Any further complaints?

Mr Ndebvu: No, Your Worship [*he sits down*].

Magistrate: Mr Prosecutor, may you please read out the allegations.

Prosecutor: [*stands up and reads from a piece of paper*]: Yes, Your Worship. The accused person is aged 24 and resides at number 10513, Third Avenue, Harare. She is facing 38 allegations of fraud or alternatively theft by false pretences. It is alleged that between 20 January and 30 March this year and in her capacity as a bank teller, she defrauded her employer, that is Barstan bank, a bank situated at 54 Samora Machel Avenue, Harare.

During the course of her employment, Your Worship, she was tasked with buying foreign currency from bank customers. Each day, she would be given a rate at which the bank would be buying diverse foreign currencies. Ordinarily, Your Worship, bank rates are displayed on an electronic board within the bank and customers can readily see the exchange rates.

However, during power cuts which this country is experiencing, the said board will not be functioning. It was during these power cuts that the accused person found opportunities to perpetrate these offences. On each count, she would misrepresent to the customers the rate at which the bank would be buying foreign currencies which in effect was lower than what the bank would have instructed her to buy at. The accused would then convert the difference between the two rates and spirit it away.

In total, Your Worship, the accused person received US$260 000. The offence came to light when her unemployed brother, one Vengai Bunda, was arrested laden with part of her loot, amounting to US$5 000. The said Vengai was arrested while boozing at an upmarket local hotel and was even extending his graciousness by plying any Tom, Dick and Harry who walked through the doors with imported, fine liquor.

The brother who has no other visible means of living in assisting the police with their investigations led them to the accused person's swanky residence where her modest salary will never, Your Worship, in hundreds of years be sufficient to purchase such upmarket property.

Through the accused person's indications, the police recovered a cache of money amounting to US$255 000 under her bed. The bank has unearthed documentary evidence linking the accused person to the offences. Those are the allegations, Your Worship.

Magistrate: [*to Busani*]: Do you understand the allegations being levelled against you, accused person?

Busani: Yes, Your Worship.

Magistrate [*to Busani*]: Very well, sit down [*Busani sits in the dock in-between two female prison officers and now and then anxiously looks into the gallery*].

Magistrate: [*to the prosecutor*]: What is the state's position as regards bail for the accused person?

Prosecutor: The state strongly opposes bail, Your Worship ... [*someone wails in the gallery*].

Magistrate: [*glares into the gallery*]: Who is that making noise in my court? Stand up!

Mrs Bunda: [*stands up on shaky legs*]: I am Busani's mother.

Magistrate: [*points at her with his gavel*]: These are courts of law; we don't like people wailing as if this is a funeral gathering [*the gallery laughs*].

Court Orderly: [*stands up and shouts*]: Silence in court! [*laughter in the gallery stops*].

Magistrate: [*to Mrs Bunda*]: Next time you disturb this court, you will join your daughter in the dock. Do you understand?

Mrs Bunda: [*staring at the floor]:* Yes.

Magistrate: [*turns to the prosecutor*]: Please continue, Mr Prosecutor.

Prosecutor: Your Worship, the state opposes bail on two grounds: the first being that she is a flight risk, that is bearing in mind that already, a vast sum of money has been recovered from beneath her own bed. She has neither laid claim to the money and nor has she given a sound explanation for such possession. Chances of her getting convicted are very high and a lengthy prison term is inevitable. She is single, with therefore nothing to lose if she takes flight.

Secondly, if she is released, she will interfere with the investigations. So far, the bank in reconciling its records, has unearthed these 38 counts. Just as I was stepping into this court, Your Worship, I received word from the bank that over a hundred more counts have been unearthed and will be added to ... [*there is commotion in the gallery as Mrs Bunda cries out and collapses*].

Magistrate: [*to the Court Orderly*]: Mr Court Orderly, please see to it she is removed from this honourable court.

Court Orderly: Yes, Your Worship [*he rises from a desk behind the bar and moves back into the gallery*].

Magistrate: [*to the prosecutor and Mr Ndebvu*]: Gentlemen, in light of this disturbance, let us adjourn.

Prosecutor: Yes, Your Worship.

Ndebvu: I agree, Your Worship.

Magistrate [*rising*]: This court adjourns!

Prosecutor: [*as the whole court rises, he shouts*]: Silence in court!

[*Exit all*].

Scene II

Opens with Mrs Bunda being supported into the court room by a relative and is led to sit at the back of the court room. Shortly the court resumes. A bell is heard within the court room.

Prosecutor: [*as everyone in the court rises, he shouts*]: Silence in court! [*the interpreter opens a door and ushers the magistrate into the court room*).

Magistrate: [*sits down and addresses the court*]: Please sit down [*the whole court sits down, and he promptly looks at Mrs Bunda in the gallery*]: Stand up! [*she unsteadily stands up*]: So, what was wrong with you?

Mrs Bunda: [*mumbling*]: I think, I fainted…I [*gallery laughs*].

Magistrate: [*sternly]*: Look here, this court has seen it all. We see through every ruse. Your attempts to sway us with cries and wailings will fall on deaf ears. We are not moved at all by such theatrics. If you know you are prone to fainting upon hearing grave news, then, please don't come to my court. Very grave things are said in this court [*gallery laughs*].

Mrs Bunda: It won't happen again.

Magistrate: [*he turns to the prosecutor*]: You may please continue, Mr Prosecutor.

Prosecutor: [*stands up*]: Yes, Your Worship. As I submitted earlier on, Your Worship, the accused is likely to face more charges as the bank digs deeper into her illicit behaviour. This breaking news, Your Worship, will spur her on to flee. That is all, Your Worship [*and he sits down*].

Magistrate: [*to the lawyer*]: Mr Ndebvu, any response?

Ndebvu: [*stands up*]: Yes, Your Worship. While I appreciate that investigations are still in their infancy as suggested by my learned friend, this initial hearing is not a determination of whether my client is guilty or not. We have not reached that stage and yet my learned friend has already crossed that bridge and in his wisdom, has already found my client guilty.

Our Constitution, Your Worship, plainly states that one is not guilty until proven so. My learned friend needs to revisit those basic tenets of fundamental human rights.

What we have heard, Your Worship, are mere bold allegations. The state's case hangs upon money recovered in my client's house and her supposed failure to account for such possession. Your Worship, my client explained her possession of the money, which explanation my learned friend here has deliberately withheld from this honourable court.

My learned friend's basic aim, Your Worship, is to besmirch my client' standing before this court. She told the bank and the investigating officer that she runs a business in partnership with a wealthy friend. Now, we all know how difficult in this current climate it is to withdraw your own money from banks. For the purpose of keeping the business running and not being hamstrung by cash flow problems, my client, in her wisdom, felt it best to keep the money in her house.

This, Your Worship is a shrewd, common practice in the business community, which my learned friend seems not privy to. The defence vehemently assert that it is her money and will fight tooth and nail to recover it. She is going nowhere until she recovers her money and any talk of her taking flight is just a fanciful imagination of the state.

Secondly, the defence *in limine*, assert that the bank is wrongly cited as the complainant. It is not the complainant *per se* [*he puts his hands in his trouser pockets and struts around the bar*].

From what we heard from the prosecution; it follows then it was the customers who were duped when they sold their foreign currency at a lower rate. The bank at the end of the day got its dues from the transactions. So, in essence, Your Worship, it is those 38 bank customers who should be complainants in this court and not the bank. The bank logically and at law suffered no prejudice, it merely wants to have a double dipping.

Unfortunately, Your Worship, none of those 38 customers have been named in this court nor has it been suggested that they have lodged complaints with the police. As such my client was pounced upon unlawfully and is still sitting in this honourable court unlawfully. I humbly submitted, Your Worship, that my learned friend is wasting this court's time and the defence therefore seeks the immediate release of my client [*he struts around the bar again*].

If, however, the court is of the view that the allegations suffice for my client to be put on remand, the defence humbly submit that she is a good candidate for bail. My learned friend here, [*he places a hand on the prosecutor' shoulder and the prosecutor shrugs him off*] however, suggests that my client is a flight-risk. If the courts were in the habit of viewing single persons as flight-risk, then our prisons, Your Worship, would be full to capacity with single persons [*gallery laughs*].

Court Orderly: [*shouts*]: Silence in court!

Ndebvu: [*turns and smiles to people in the gallery and then turns back to face the magistrate*]: Your Worship, though the gallery is supposed to listen quietly, they equally find the assertion that because my client is single, she will definitely flee laughable [*he pauses*]:

We have been informed that all the money was recovered and in the unlikely event that a court of law convicts my client, it is very unlikely that she will be sent to prison in light of previous sentences by our higher courts in respect of women. Therefore, there is nothing to prompt her to flee.

My learned friend here, [*he points a finger at the prosecutor*] has sought to magnify the charges by asserting that more counts have been unearthed. He even called it breaking news. One wonders why the state notwithstanding getting more damning information against my client nonetheless chose to come to court with these fewer charges [*he wags a figure at the prosecutor*]. My learned friend, is not being honest with this court. The court can balance the interests of justice and my client's liberty by granting her bail with strict conditions.

In sum, Your Worship, the defence urges the court to rule that the wrong complainant has been cited here and unless those 38 persons allegedly duped by my client make formal complaints, my client should be released forthwith. However, if the court is of the view that the allegations suffice to put my client on remand, the defence suggests stringent bail conditions as follows. The first condition being that she be admitted to bail in the sum of $10 000 bond notes and secondly that she reports thrice a week at CID Frauds in Harare and thirdly, she surrenders her passport to the clerk of court. Fourthly, that my client resides at her home until this matter is finalised. That is all, Your Worship, unless the court wishes the defence to address it on other aspects of this matter.

Magistrate: Thank you defence counsel [*Mr Ndebvu sits down*]: Mr Prosecutor, any reply?

Prosecutor: [*stands up*]: Yes, Your Worship, the state wishes to make a reply.

Magistrate: [*to the prosecutor*]: Very well, let us adjourn for lunch and we will hear the state's response after the break if both parties are available.

Prosecutor: Yes, Your Worship [*he sits down*].

Magistrate: [*to the lawyer*]: Mr Ndebvu shall we resume in the afternoon?

Ndebvu: [*stands up*]: Yes, Your worship.

Magistrate: [*stands up*]: This court adjourns!

Prosecutor: [*shouts*]: Silence in court!

[Exit all].

Scene III

Takes place in the magistrate's office where the magistrate and the interpreter are engaged in a conversation.

Magistrate: [*to the interpreter*]: Well, my friend, I deliberately stopped the proceedings before the prosecutor could reply for two reasons. Firstly, I wanted that accused person, her family and friends to feel the enormity of the case.

Interpreter: [*beaming, he handshakes the magistrate*]: Very good timing, Your Worship!

Magistrate: Secondly, I didn't know what the prosecutor was going to say because the defence has raised some important legal and factual points especially as regards who should stand as the complainant. Who knows, the prosecutor might have agreed right there in court with the defence, and off, our bird would have flown away!

Interpreter: That is a possibility which we should guard against very jealously, Your Worship.

Magistrate: Tell them, I will grant the accused person bail this afternoon on the conditions suggested by the lawyer. So, you need to get our money during this lunch hour before the prosecutor responds.

Interpreter: So, how much should they cough up?

Magistrate: This is a big one my friend, tell them it is very risky. Get us US$50 000.

Interpreter: [*stands up*]: Okay. I will have a chat with the brother. It should be easy to make them see the hazard.

[*Exit all*].

Scene IV

Takes place in the foyer of the court room, where Busani's relatives are engaged in a conversation. The interpreter beckons Vengai aside.

Interpreter: This is a big, very tricky case my brother.

Vengai: Don't worry, my brother, money is not a problem at all. Just name the figure.

Interpreter: He wants US$100 000.

Vengai: Give me a minute [*he moves aside and makes a phone call to Nomsa using his mobile phone*]: Hi.

Nomsa: [*on her mobile*]: Hi, my brother, any fruitful developments?

Vengai: I am right now standing next to the intermediary, that is the interpreter. He said money moves mountains, but it is going to be expensive to do so, my sister. They want US$150 000.

Nomsa: That is quite a lot, but never mind, the cash is only a stone throw away. We want the best for your sister.

Vengai: Thanks a million, I will ring you back soon [*he hangs up and moves back to where the interpreter is standing*].

Interpreter: Well?

Vengai: My friends have been shocked by your demands. They asked if the magistrate could take US$50, 000.

Interpreter: [*sniggers*]: You must be joking! Have you considered what will happen to the magistrate if this corrupt enterprise blows up in his face?

Vengai: No, my brother.

Interpreter: Okay, let me tell you. The magistrate will go to prison. Even if he manages somehow to cling to dear life in prison, his career in law will evaporate overnight. Who will then feed his family? Would a mere US$50 000 in this expensive Zimbabwe see to that?

Vengai: Okay, I understand what you are saying. I am confident though that we will be able to raise the required sum over this lunch break. So how will I pass the money to you?

Interpreter: Do you know a pub called the *Beer Engine* situated in the city centre?

Vengai: [*laughs*]: I know all pubs in Harare!

Interpreter: [*sneers*]: I should not have asked given your reputation as outlined in court. Meet me there in 30 minutes time.

Vengai: Ok, please help my sister.

Interpreter: [*sternly*]: Don't try anything funny like setting a police trap for me.

Vengai: [*taken aback*]: Not at all, my bother. Let us swop phone numbers.

Interpreter: Good idea [*they swop phone numbers*]: See you soon.

Vengai: Let me rush to get the cash [*exit*].

Interpreter: [*30 minutes later at the Beer Engine, he calls Vengai on his mobile*]: Are you coming or not as it is nearly time for the afternoon court session?

Vengai: [*on his mobile phone*]: My apologies my good brother, I am running late due to heavy traffic. I have the money though.

Interpreter: How long will it take you to get here?

Vengai: Another 30 minutes, I think.

Interpreter: I have to ring the magistrate first and get back to you.

Vengai: Okay, my brother.

Interpreter: [*calls the magistrate on his mobile phone*]: They have the money, but they are running late by 30 minutes, what must I do?

Magistrate: Let us give them time to arrange our money. Come back to court and I will postpone the matter to tomorrow.

Interpreter: Okay [*he calls Vengai on his mobile*]: I have to go now; we have set times to sit in court. Your sister's matter will be postponed to tomorrow. We can't set her free without you playing your part.

Vengai: [*pleadingly*]: My brother, we are honest people, set her free this afternoon and I will hand the money to you later today.

Interpreter: [*laughs*]: Only a fool will accede to such an arrangement in Harare. By the nature of this transaction, if you fail to deliver, we cannot send debt collectors after you. Meet me here after the court session [*exits*].

Vengai: [*soliloquises*]: Who needs to be a banker? I have just earned myself a cool US$50 000 in less than an hour [*exit*].

Scene V

Scene opens in the court room with the matter of the State versus Busani Bunda being heard.

Magistrate: [*to the prosecutor*]: Mr Prosecutor, you said before we adjourned that the state wished to respond to Mr Ndebvu' submissions.

Prosecutor: [*stands up*]: Yes, Your Worship, I wish to reply.

Magistrate: Well, I am sorry Mr Prosecutor and defence counsel to say that there is an urgent matter which I have to attend to involving the administration of justice. Consequently, we have to postpone this matter. If both parties are available tomorrow, we can resume the hearing in the morning at 09:30.

Prosecutor: [*confers with Mr Ndebvu seated next to him and responds to the magistrates*]: In agreement with my learned friend, Your Worship, we will avail ourselves at 9: 30 tomorrow [*he sits down*].

Magistrate: Very well, stand up accused person [*Busani stands up*]. We don't have time to hear this matter further today. Come back tomorrow, you will be remanded in custody.

Busani: [*shocked*]: In prison?

Magistrate: Yes, your lawyer will appraise you on that.

Ndebvu: [*stands up*]: Yes, Your Worship, I will have a conversation with her [*he sits down*].

Magistrate: [*rising up*]: Very well, this court adjourns.

Prosecutor: [*stands up together with Mr Ndebvu and he shouts*]: Silence in court! [*the whole court stands up and the interpreter as per custom opens the door for the magistrate and they exit*].

Interpreter: [*chuckling*]. A very wise move indeed, Your Worship.

Magistrate: [*smiles*]: We are the masters of deception in Harare, my friend. Meet the brother and get our money. For obvious reasons, I can't come to the *Beer Engine* with you.

Interpreter: No problem, Your Worship.

Magistrate: Ring me as soon as you get our money.

Interpreter: No problem, Your Worship.

[*Exit both*].

Scene VI

Meanwhile in the prosecutor's office, the prosecutor, the investigating officer and John are engaged in a conversation.

Prosecutor: We need to put pressure on these thieving bankers. That technicality, that the bank is not the complainant in this matter could cause a problem.

John: [*vehemently*]: But surely the bank is the complainant.

Prosecutor: [*to John*] It's an arguable point. We need therefore to cover every loophole.

I.O: [*to the prosecutor*]: Can I do anything to help? My officer in charge is expecting nothing less than a conviction in this matter.

Prosecutor: [*laughs*]: All is not lost, gentlemen. You have to work together on this matter, overnight.

I.O: No problem, this is a big case; I might get promoted should we nail this thieving, shameless woman.

Prosecutor: [*to John*]: How many bank customers can you get this afternoon to lay charges against the accused person?

John: That is not a problem, most clients who were duped conduct business in the city centre. A number of them thronged the bank when this matter was heralded in the media. They expressed their eagerness to claw back their loses. I can easily get ten to lay charges against Busani by the end of this day.

Prosecutor: That is brilliant. John, you need then to work with the investigating officer to get those clients to lay charges against Busani.

John: No problem, Mr Prosecutor.

Prosecutor: [*he turns to the investigating officer*]: Armed with the names of those bank clients; please prepare fresh allegations against Busani, opposing the granting of bail strongly. Bring the papers to my office by nine tomorrow morning.

I.O: [*smiles*]: No problem at all, Mr Prosecutor. This won't be an easy walk to freedom for that fraudster.

Prosecutor: Okay, this is our strategy gentlemen. If the court dismisses the allegations against the accused person in that the bank is not the complainant tomorrow, I want you as the investigating officer to wait for her outside the remand prison.

As soon as Busani sets foot outside the prison, quickly curtail her freedom, arrest and cart her to the police station [*he smiles*]. I will be very keen to hear what submissions our Mr Ndebvu will come up with when she next appears in court with the injured bank clients being the complainants. We will unlikely see our esteemed lawyer strutting as he did today. I promise you gentlemen, Busani will experience in prison what Nelson Mandela meant, by a long walk to freedom.

John: [*vigorously handshakes the prosecutor*]: An absolutely brilliant strategy!

I.O: [*beaming*]: Mr Prosecutor, I like the way you close every avenue of escape. I am very impressed.

Prosecutor: [*smiles*]: That is the difference between lay persons and us in the legal fraternity.

I.O: Mr Prosecutor, I must mention that your prowess is the talk of the police force.

John: [*to the investigating officer*]: He is the man to sort out these thieves. I think that after sending all the fraudsters at the bank where they should be, that is in prison, Mr Prosecutor must head either ZACC or SACU and sweep the vermin that is bleeding this dear country to its knees.

I.O: Indeed!

Prosecutor: [*smiles*]: Off you go gentlemen, you have work to do. Keep me posted.

John: I will.

I.O: Bye, Mr Prosecutor. I will be here well before you open your office.

Prosecutor: See you both.

[*Exit all*].

ACT III

Scene I

Opens at the Beer Engine, where the interpreter and Vengai are seated at a table. Unknown to them, Ashton, a bank security officer seated in a far corner is observing them.

Interpreter: Do you have it all?

Vengai: Yes [*he produces a satchel which he places on the table and starts to open it*].

Interpreter: [*glances around furtively*]: Don't open it; you don't know who is watching.

Vengai: Sorry my brother.

Interpreter: [*makes a mobile phone call*]: Drive up to the door now, a gentleman in an orange jacket is coming out now with the package [*he finishes his call and turns to Vengai*]. To obviate surprises, you are not going to hand me that satchel in here. Rather, give it to a driver wearing a yellow shirt and seated in a yellow Nissan Micra parked outside this pub. The driver will ring me to confirm delivery. Okay?

Vengai: Okay [*he exits carrying the satchel*].

Interpreter: [*makes a mobile call to the magistrate*]: I am just waiting to hear from the courier to confirm delivery.

Magistrate: [*on his mobile phone*]: That cousin of yours would definitely outwit even the much-acclaimed James Bond. His role has suited us very well in the past. Keep me posted [*he switches off*].

Enter Vengai

Vengai: [*sits next to the interpreter*]: I have given your friend the money, but what if he tricks you?

Interpreter: My friend, don't worry about that. We are not fools at all. We have been in this game for a long, long time. We have the utmost trust in that driver. He has served our purposes well in the past.

Vengai: Sorry, I just wanted to be sure because I need my sister to be released soonest.

Interpreter: [*gulps his beer*]: My brother, we have learnt from the mistakes of other court officials. We have perfected the game.

Vengai: How, my brother?

Interpreter: [*gloats*]: We think on our feet. For example, in the afternoon, the driver was not needed as it was going to be impossible for anyone to set a trap against us given, we were set to meet in 30 minutes time.

When the police set up a trap to catch criminals, there are legal procedures that they have to follow and these take time. But now there has been sufficient time to set such a trap to arrest us and I therefore devised a strategy to outwit the police in this matter.

Vengai: Surely, I would not do that to you.

Interpreter: [*slurring, he brags*]. We have polished our act my friend like *Eneke*, the bird in Chinua Achebe's *Things Fall Apart* book.

Vengai: What did the bird do?

Interpreter: Oh, you don't know, do you? Well, Achebe wrote that *Eneke* in noting that men had learnt to shoot without missing their mark, the bird then also learnt to fly without perching. [*He quaffs his beer and points at himself*]: We, the dealers in Harare, have become adepts at equally evading being shot down. We act in cahoots with the police.

Only a senior policeman authorises a trap and procedurally, he instructs a junior officer to type the order. But my friend [*he laughs*], those junior officers before even typing a single word, they phone us, warning of the impending trap. So, who is clever? Of course, it's us!

Vengai: So, you are saying definitely my sister will walk free tomorrow?

Interpreter: You see... [*his mobile phone rings and he answers it*]: That is fine cousin, I will see you later.

Vengai: Your cousin confirming that I gave him the money?

Interpreter: Yes. Can you buy me more beer my brother; all that money is for the magistrate.

Vengai: No problem [*he pushes a ward of US$20 notes into the interpreter's pocket*].

Interpreter: Thanks, my brother from my other mother.

Vengai: You are welcome.

Interpreter: [*looking around the pub*]: You have to go now, my friend, Harare has many eyes.

Vengai: Okay, see you tomorrow [*he gulps down all the beer in his glass and exits*].

Interpreter: [*soliloquises*]: This is Harare, a city where one grows fat without the need to be learned. There is no need at all for a law degree; any fool can earn serious money here. I have just earned myself US50 000 and His Worship with his law degree won't even know of the deception. So, tell me, who then is the master of deception? [*he beats his chest with his clenched fist*]: Me of course! [*he raises his hand, a signal to the barman to bring him more beer*].

Ashton: [*seated in a far corner of the pub, he rings John*]: Boss, you are a true detective. Your intuition has paid off. I followed Vengai into in the *Beer Engine* where he met the court interpreter. He then tried to hand him a satchel, but the interpreter refused to take it. Shortly then, Vengai went outside the bar with the satchel and returned without it.

John: [*laughs*]: It is the middlemen who receive the money for the corrupt people in Harare. That satchel contained a payment for the magistrate. No one can link the magistrate directly to the exchange. They know how to play the game.

Ashton: [*sighs*]: So, she is going to be released?

John: Don't worry, I have that covered.

[*Exit all*].

Scene II

Opens at a city centre pub that same night, John and the prosecutor are having alcoholic drinks.

John: My junior, whom I had tasked with following Vengai with the hope of recovering more money, rung me with an update an hour ago. Apparently, Vengai met the interpreter and gave him a satchel.

Prosecutor: Really?

John: Yes. I suspect the satchel contained money destined for the magistrate.

Prosecutor: Don't worry about that. She will not set foot outside that infamous prison. Why don't you arrange for more beer to be brought here?

John: [*laughs*]: You worry unnecessarily about beer! Do I not work for a bank? I have a big allowance to entertain those who can help us to recoup our losses.

Prosecutor: [*smiles*]: Now that you said you have a huge allowance to entertain me, can we, my friend, change from these local lagers to imported waters?

John: No problem. But I think it is time to tighten the screws on the other bank tellers. If the magistrate succeeds in granting bail, they will deal with him knowing that they will never be incarcerated upon arrest.

Prosecutor: You have a point there. We need to inspire fear. We need to act very fast and show all and sundry that it is the prosecution side that is calling the shots.

John: That is right. Her fellow thieving comrades who could not attend court today are very unsettled over the overnight sleep of Busani at the dreaded remand prison. They want to meet and have conversations with me.

Prosecutor: I suppose they want their stricken friend to be released or to be assured that the long arm of the law will spare them.

John: That's right. So, back to our plan, how much should they give us?

Prosecutor: You know their purses best.

John: Given the way they have been buying properties and importing flashy cars, they must be laden with cash. I will demand the sum of US$300 000 from them.

Prosecutor: Is that sum wholly for the state?

John: Of course, it is for you. These are clever thieves; they know the Harare way. Without making any demands upon them, they have already gifted me with copious amounts of US dollars.

Prosecutor: [*smiles*]: Excellent, but perhaps, you could urge them to be more liberal, my friend.

John: To be frank with you, the bank does not know for how long this has been going on and how much was siphoned off. We know these tellers using the same method as Busani, defrauded the bank and brought properties which they registered in the names of their relatives.

Prosecutor: Is that so?

John: Yes. Let me go and meet them now and I will ring you later tonight.

[*Exit both*].

Scene III

Opens in a trendy bar in the city of Harare, the same night, where John is engaged in a conversation with bank tellers.

John: Hi, guys how are things?

Tom: Hi, John. You know very well how we are feeling. The arrest of Busani and the direction the matter has taken at court is very frightening.

Nomsa: [*looking very worried*]: I can't eat nor sleep since her arrest.

John: Well, she is asleep now at prison.

Jimmy: Look, John, your investigations are likely to net many people...

John: [*interrupts him*] There is no element of likelihood here my friends. Definitely from my investigations, more bank tellers will be arrested. The police investigating officer himself is under pressure from the bank and his superiors to show results and by results, they mean more arrests like yesterday.

Tom: [*wide-eyed*]: Oh, my God!

John: You may not know how the police carry out their investigations, so I will shed some light, from my experience. They arrest to make investigations. You have heard, I suppose, that they beat and torture suspects with some, even dying in police cells.

To be honest with you guys, many bank tellers are going to be residents of Chikurubi Maximum Security Prison for long, long periods. I urge those involved to eat as much pizzas and dine at the much-fancied Nando's as much as they can before they

51

get nabbed. At Chikurubi, there is no adequate food. If recent reports are true, inmates last had meat three years ago.

Tom: Well, who are your suspects?

John: We don't want people panicking unnecessarily. But we have substantial information about both movable and immovable properties bought by bank staff well beyond their means.

But even then, if there is no evidence of fraudulent acts by a teller at the bank, we will definitely engage ZACC and SACU to sniff around. It is unlikely that after casting their nets wide, these efficient organisations will fail to catch anyone. Some bank tellers will definitely be caught out. Mark my words [*he takes a swig at his beer*].

Nomsa: Oh, my God!

John: We discovered that many bank tellers do not reside at the addresses which they gave to the bank. For example, one gave her home as being in Mabvuku, a high-density area, but apparently, she lives in the upmarket Borrowdale area. Interestingly, the property is registered in her uncle's name, who himself is a long-time pauper and a rural dweller. So, questions will be asked and answers will be required.

Nomsa: [*cries out*]: Oh, my God!

John: [*ignoring her*]: Checks at the title deeds office have unearthed shocking evidence. Of course, some of the relatives may vehemently insist that they bought the properties using their own legitimate funds. However, my friends, our police force is renowned for causing people to loosen their tongues. You have heard the police saying on numerous occasions that, 'we are not going to fold our hands while crime is happening'. If necessary, they break bones to solve crimes. It is an old-fashioned way, but it works. Sometimes they take suspects and throw them down disused, dark mine shafts and ...

Nomsa: [*trembling*]: Oh, my God, stop saying that!

John: [*sipping his beer*]: These are interesting times my friends.

Tom: Okay, so what can we do?

Jimmy: Good question, Tom. That is why we are all here, to chart an amicable course.

John: Okay, I have spoken to the right persons so that your friend could be released.

Nomsa: [*pleadingly*]: Oh, thank you, John.

John: It will take a substantial amount to make these people look the other way.

Tom: How much?

John: US$300 000 only.

Jimmy: [*aghast*]: Ah! We don't have that kind of money!

Nomsa: We have already given $150 000 to Busani's brother.

Jimmy: Yes, Vengai took our money this afternoon after telling us that his sister's loot had all been taken away by the police and we have to help his sister.

John: Indeed, the eagle-eyed Ashton did observe Vengai handing money to the interpreter for onward delivery to the magistrate. However, you placed a bet on the wrong horse, my friends. It is only the prosecutor who can deliver the results you anxiously need.

Tom: But US$300 000 really? That is more than what the prosecutor will earn in decades.

Jimmy: That is right, we process their salaries and the demand is preposterous. He will not get that much from us. Never!

John: So how much can you cough?

Tom: I am tired of paying corrupt people.

Jimmy: I think US$50 000 will do.

Tom: Guys, I am leaving. I have had enough of this extortion [*he grabs his jacket and rises to go*].

Jimmy: [*to Tom*]: Come on Tom. This is a serious matter. You can't just walk away. We are in this together.

Nomsa: Please Tom, don't go, Busani needs us.

Tom: Can you not see that everyone is bent on milking us.

John: [*stands up*]: It is up to you guys. We shall see if your friend will be released tomorrow. However, think about this scenario; if your friend's bid for freedom fails tomorrow and the gaol keys are thrown away, do you seriously believe she will languish in the dungeons in silence, knowing some fraudulent tellers are living cushy lives? From my experience in the police force, I am pessimistic that she will lump it.

Nomsa: Busani is our friend, she won't betray us.

John: [*laughs*]: My friends, we may say you know more about business law but you know nothing about criminal law. The courts pass lenient sentences to crooks who help out in the conviction of other offenders. Many convicts reduce their time in prison by snitching. Busani will start singing sooner than you think. Anyway, goodbye, drink as much as you can, for who knows for how long some of you will be free to savour those exotic waters [*exit*].

Nomsa: Oh, Jesus! I don't know what to do now.

Tom: Let us wait and see. I have faith in the magistrate route. After all, that building is called Harare Magistrates Court, not Harare Prosecutors Court.

Jimmy: I agree with you Tom, let us wait and see.

Nomsa: [*sobbing*]: Oh, my God. The wheels are coming off. This is the end of us.

Tom: [*consoling her*]: Don't worry my dear; it is who will have the last laugh. Stealing the money was the hard part.

Jimmy: Quite right Tom. It just needs us to put money in the right pocket and all will end superbly.

Tom: The problem with Harare is that when people smell money, they all want a share of it.

Nomsa: Don't worry, darling, all will be okay.

Tom: You think so?

Nomsa: Fingers crossed.

[*Exit all*].

Scene IV

Opens the same day, late at night in the magistrate's lounge where the magistrate and the interpreter are quaffing beers.

Magistrate [*smiles*]: Well done, for executing this one, my good friend.

Interpreter: [*smiles*]: Some institution should surely honour me with a doctorate degree in these matters!

Magistrate: [*laughs*]: I heard there are some institutions in town honouring certain people for their good deeds. Also, there is a small island somewhere in the world offering doctorate degrees!

Interpreter: [*laughs*]: Hardly will my ill deeds qualify for an honorary doctorate!

Magistrate: [*laughs*]: It is not going to happen; you have to go to a proper university. Anyway, how much did you manage to get from them?

Interpreter: [*brings out from his satchel, bundles of US dollars and places them on the table*]: As per His Worship's demand, they gave me US$50 000.

Magistrate: [*licks his lips and reaches for the bundles*]: Good! I thought they would settle for less.

Interpreter: I pressed upon them the dire consequences of seeking out your help and then refusing to play ball.

Magistrate: You do amuse me with how you scare people in our court through the medium of speech.

Interpreter: [*laughs*]: If we interpret in a dry manner, people will go to sleep. It is an art of the trade.

Magistrate: Back to business, how much do you want?

Interpreter: The usual ratio will be great, Your Worship.

Magistrate: Our usual ratio would give you something like US$16 000 but take US$20 000 for a job well done.

Interpreter: [*picks up his share*]: Thanks. You don't know how much I appreciate this.

Magistrate: I know you guys are not paid much. I have often said to you, my friend, that I will make you rich as long as you bring business.

Interpreter: [*smiles*]: Your Worship, I will scout for business every court day and after hours and even over the weekend.

Magistrate: Bring all the business you can, and I will sort it out.

Interpreter: [*stands up*]: Given the dream of owning my own house, business will keep streaming your way. Anyway, I have to go now, my cousin is waiting outside.

Magistrate: Take care. I will be late for court tomorrow as I need to pay fees for my kids lest they get kicked out of the boarding school. I will also need to clear my rent arrears with my landlord and lastly pay the garage for them to release my car. If that accused person's friends and relatives become pests, tell them to relax as she will be released without fail today.

On another note, I suspect that those bankrolling her bid for freedom had a hand in this criminal enterprise. We could be sitting on a gold mine, my friend. They need to be assured that I am here for them and so there is no need for them to flee our beautiful country.

Interpreter: [*exiting*]: You are right. Her workmates are all suspects. Good night! [*exit*].

Magistrate: [*soliloquises*]: This young interpreter is the top man. All my debts are settled, leaving me with some change. Can you imagine a magistrate's kids being kicked out of a boarding school for want of fees? [*He beats his chest using his hand*]: My mother didn't raise up a fool, just as the legendary Tu Pac sang. I will twist the law to suit my needs [*exit*].

Interpreter: [*soliloquises on his way out*]: I now have US70 000 and his Worship, a mere US$30 000. No matter how tough things get in this country, Harare will always provide food for the agile minded. There is, therefore no need whatsoever, to go abroad or to the so-called diaspora. I love this city [*exit*].

ACT IV

Scene I

The scene opens with the prosecutor addressing the court in the matter of the State versus Busani Bunda the next day.

Prosecutor: In response to my learned friend's address yesterday in which he lamely suggested that the bank is not the complainant, it is humbly submitted Your Worship, that it is indeed the rightful complainant. We have not reached that stage yet where the defence can aver that the charge is defective in that a wrong complainant has been cited. That is a procedure reserved for trials, not bail applications.

Already, ten complainants have lodged reports against the accused person and as such the complainants may change as investigations are carried out. What we have at this stage are thousands of US dollars recovered from the accused person and she could not account for that money. It has been suggested that it is her legitimate money, but Your Worship, it is expected that a banker involved in a business, would exhibit business acumen in her conducting business.

It is, therefore laughable, Your Worship, that the supposed businesswoman in the person of the accused person and more so in a business partnership would shower her alcoholic brother with money meant for business purposes. So loaded was Vengai, Your Worship, that he is well famed with stupefying numerous high end club patrons with free liquor. I do not believe, nor should the court be led to believe that the accused person would be so reckless with money from a genuine business partnership. This money, Your Worship, was obtained illicitly during the course of her duties at the bank. So, for the court to let her walk away now, would be a travesty of justice.

I do not wish to address the court on the matter of bail conditions; the state's position hasn't changed at all. Bail is still strongly opposed. Unless they are issues which the court wishes the state to address it on, that is all in response to my learned friend' submissions [*he sits down*].

Magistrate: Mr Ndebvu, any response to Mr prosecutor' submissions.

Ndebvu: [*stands up*]: Yes, Your Worship. The state is jumping all over the place, Your Worship. We now hear of 10 people who have lodged complaints against my innocent client but the complainant cited in this case and currently, is the bank. It does not matter, and the court should not be persuaded by supposed and fanciful breaking news from my learned friend that millions of people aggrieved by my client's lawful conduct of banking business are in snaking queues waiting to press charges against her at police stations within Zimbabwe and abroad.

The defence is not moved at all and urge the court not to be misled by such submissions as those alleged complainants' cases are not before his honourable court. *In casu*, the state should put its house in order first and not waste this court's time jumping left and right. The defence insists and demands that this honourable court sets the accused person free as she is in a wrong place and at a wrong time. That is all, Your Worship [*he sits down*].

Magistrate: Very well. I am retiring to write my ruling and will deliver it, say at 2:15 pm, if the time suits both parties.

Prosecutor: [*confers with Mr Ndebvu seated next to him and then addresses the magistrate*]: The time is convenient to the state and the defence, Your Worship.

Magistrate: [*rising*]: This court adjourns!

Prosecutor: [*shouts*]: Silence in court! [*the whole court stands up, exchanges the customary bows with the magistrate who then exits with the interpreter. Busani is led away to the court's holding cells by a prison officer*].

Ndebvu: [*to the prosecutor*]: What is really your problem, Mr Prosecutor? Do you have some vested interests in this matter?

Prosecutor: Are you implying something?

Ndebvu: For you to vehemently oppose bail based on spurious grounds, it raises in my legal experience, some serious questions about your professionalism.

Prosecutor: [*smiles*]: You old guys are ever bragging about your glorious past experiences. Look here, history has shown that in my court, you have always left without your clients as they are taken to jail. I suggest you see a shrink.

Ndebvu: [*sniggers*]: Always check the demeanour of your magistrate when you address a court, my learned friend. It will save you time and energy and as of now, the magistrate is laughing in your face. Can you not see that?

Prosecutor: Heaven help us if we are now to judge a court's upcoming verdict by reading a magistrate's face [*exit*].

Ndebvu: [*as he leaves the court, he is surrounded by Busani's relatives and addresses them*]: The magistrate has gone, as you heard, to write his judgement. So, come back for the next session at 2 pm.

Mrs Busani: Mr Ndebvu, do you think she will be released?

Ndebvu: The prosecution has not presented a case at all. I am very confident that the magistrate will throw this case away today.

Mrs Busani: Thank you so much sir. Thank you for the good work.

Ndebvu: Don't thank me yet.

[Exit all].

Scene II

In the prosecutor's office, the prosecutor, the investigating officer and John are engaged in a conversation.

John: Mr Prosecutor, what do you think will be the ruling on this bail issue?

Prosecutor: I think he is going to grant her bail. He did seem uninterested in my reply.

I.O: Could you not have called someone from the bank to explain in detail how the bank fits as the complainant?

Prosecutor: [*smiles*]: Officer, I know what I am doing. Calling a witness would not have added value to my argument. In any event, we need to bring you up to date with what has been happening behind the scenes.

I.O: A sixth sense tells me that something is afoot.

John: That maybe so, officer. Yesterday, my assistant saw the interpreter and the accused person's brother at the *Beer Engine*. Those two had no good cause to meet there. Vengai passed a big satchel which we strongly believe contained money meant for the magistrate.

I.O: Do you want me to arrest all of them now?

Prosecutor: At this stage, there is no evidence to suggest that someone has been corrupt. So just chill, go for your lunch and we meet in court.

I.O: Okay but if you need me to pounce on anyone at any time, just point out the culprit and it will be game over for that individual. We still have plenty of space to accommodate thieves at the police station [*exit*].

Prosecutor: These are the type of police officers we need in this country.

John: Indeed. As I said yesterday, those bank tellers said they are putting their trust in the magistrate and will not give you even a penny.

Prosecutor: You worry unnecessarily, John. I have a few tricks up my sleeve, just wait and see.

John: We can't let this chance slip away.

Prosecutor: [*laughs*]: It is not going to happen.

[*Exit both*].

Scene III

Opens in the court room with the magistrate delivering his ruling in the matter of the State versus Busani Bunda.

Magistrate: [*to Busani*]: Stand up accused person and listen carefully to this court's ruling [*Busani stands up in the dock in-between two prison officers*]: You were brought here for an initial remand, charged with fraud, alternatively theft by false pretences.

It was alleged by the state that during the course of your duties as a bank teller, you defrauded your employer of US$260 000. The state contended that you did this by buying foreign currency from bank customers at a lower rate than what the bank had authorised you to do. Further, it was alleged that you were found in possession of the fruits of the fraud hidden under your bed and some of it was recovered from your brother.

While the state suggested it is the proceeds of fraud from the bank, you contended through your lawyer that the money is actually yours. The defence asserted that the bank is not the complaint in this matter but persons who made transactions with you. This court agrees with the defence that it is the bank customers who were allegedly duped and not the bank. However, those persons have not been cited in this court as the complainants. Further, these bank customers have not laid charges against you. The bank cannot be said at law to be the complainant in this case.

However, the court takes cognisant of the fact that substantial money was recovered from an unlikely place. Whereas, bankers expect ordinary persons to take their savings to banks, it is against this received wisdom we find you, a banker, storing large sums of money under your bed. Your brother equally was plying the city's imbibers with free liquor and it is him who led the police to you.

The court will not be hoodwinked into believing a business, especially one run by a banker, would dole out money in such a manner to their relatives, no matter how close they are. The defence has merely asserted that the money belongs to a business partnership in which the accused person is party to. However, that partner was not called as a witness to add weight to the assertion or lay claim to that money. The court is not persuaded by the defence that you should be released scot-free.

I am persuaded at this stage that the facts in as much as they do not support an allegation of fraud, they do support an allegation of theft. The prosecution has indicated that 38 people were duped but erred in not citing their names. I am however not persuaded that it is a serious defect at this stage. In the circumstances, there is reasonable suspicion that you committed an offence and you must be placed on remand while investigations are being conducted.

However, the court must strike a balance between society's interests and the liberty of the accused person. There is nothing much that the state has put forward to suggest that the accused is a flight risk; all the money has been recovered. In the circumstances, the court grants the accused person bail on the conditions sought by the defence counsel.

Mrs Bunda: [*lifting her hands to the heavens*]: Oh, praise the Lord! [*stands up and begin to sing in the gallery*]: We got a reason to praise the Lord! We got a reason to praise the Lord!

Magistrate: [*directs a prison officer*]: Officer, take that woman into the holding cells and release her at the end of the day. This court has had enough of her antics.

Prison Officer: Yes, Your Worship! [*she rushes into the gallery and grabs and drags Mrs Bunda past Busani into the holding cells*].

Busani: [*wails*]: Mama! Mama!

Magistrate: [*sternly to Mr Ndebvu*]: Mr Ndebvu, may you please admonish your client. This is not a circus.

Mr Ndebvu: [*stands up*]: My apologies, Your Worship [*he walks to the dock and whispers to Busani who is seen to nod her head and he walks back to the bar*]: Your Worship, my client offers her apologies; she will henceforth hold herself with decorum.

Back to the matter before this court, while the defence is grateful, the defence contends that the court has erred by suggesting that my client be held under an allegation where no complainant has been cited. With respect, Your Worship, the court's decision is grossly wrong.

Magistrate: Mr Ndebvu, I have already made my ruling, if you wish, you may appeal against the decision to the High Court.

Mr Ndebvu: [*he hesitates for a moment*]: The defence will not pursue that line of argument any further, Your Worship.

Magistrate: Very well, the accused person is granted bail on the terms suggested by the defence. [*He looks at Busani*]: Accused person, you are to deposit $10 000 bond notes with the clerk of court and also surrender your passport to the clerk of court. You are to reside at your home until this matter is finalised. You are to report three times a week at the CID Fraud Squad headquarters in Harare on Mondays, Wednesdays and Fridays between 8 a.m. and 5 p.m. once you are released.

Failure to do as ordered, will result in your immediate arrest. If you fail to give a satisfactory account for breaching the bail conditions, you will experience the full wrath of the law. Given that you are represented, your lawyer will probably explain the consequences. Do you understand?

Busani: [*smiles*]: Yes, Your Worship.

Ndebvu: [*to the magistrate*]: I am obliged, Your Worship [*and he sits down*].

Magistrate: [*to the prosecutor*]: Mr Prosecutor, to which date shall we remand this matter to?

Prosecutor: [*stands up*]: In fact, Your Worship, the state is aggrieved by your ruling and would like to seek the views of the Prosecutor General with regard to the granting of bail. In essence, the state would like to invoke the provisions of section 121 of the Criminal Procedure and Evidence Act.

Magistrate: [*smiling*]: Come now, Mr Prosecutor do you really think the Prosecutor General will entertain your request?

Prosecutor: This is a grave matter, involving hundreds of thousands and could run into millions of US dollars. I need my superior's opinion, Your Worship.

Mr Ndebvu: [*stands up and the prosecutor sits down*]: Your Worship, the defence is anxious to have this matter resolved today and has a proposition.

Magistrate: What is your proposition, Mr Ndebvu?

Mr Ndebvu: The defence is prepared to have this matter stood down while my learned friend consults the Prosecutor General. That way, we will get a swift response today than to wait for seven days to hear his decision [*he sits down*].

Magistrate: Mr Prosecutor, would you wish to have a word with the Prosecutor General to find his opinion today or do you want now to invoke the provisions of the section right away. I hope the state understands the shaky ground of its allegations as regards the bank as the complainant.

Also, I urge the state to take cognisant of the fact that our remand prison is bursting at the seams with inmates and that judges have now and then called upon the lower courts to deny accused persons bail only in exceptional cases.

Prosecutor: [*stands up*]: Could we take a short adjournment, Your Worship?

Magistrate: [*to Busani*]: Accused person, for your benefit, the prosecutor wishes to consult his superior, that is the Prosecutor General over the court's ruling regarding the grant of bail. If a prosecutor is aggrieved by a magistrate's decision in granting bail, he or she can appeal against such a decision. If he appeals, any magistrate's hands are tied, meaning the bail which I have granted you is frozen for 7 days and you will be in remanded in custody.

If, however, the Prosecutor General indicates to the prosecutor that he consents to the granting of bail, you will be released on the bail. But if the Prosecutor General wishes to contest the granting of bail, you will remain in custody until the matter is finalised by a judge in the High Court.

However, the prosecutor has sought an adjournment to contact the Prosecutor General right away. If his boss says you are to be granted bail, you will not have to wait for seven days. So, we are going to stop these proceedings now and your lawyer will explain further if you don't understand.

Busani: [*looks fearfully at the prosecutor*]: Yes, Your Worship.

Magistrate: [*to the prosecutor*]: Very well, Mr Prosecutor, let us adjourn and when you are ready, kindly inform us. This court adjourns! [*the whole court rises*].

Prosecutor: [shouts]: Silence in court!

[*Exit all*].

Scene IV

Opens at an open space outside the court building with the interpreter surrounded by Busani's angry relatives and friends.

Interpreter: [*to the mob*]: You need to calm down or else all will be lost. There is no need for all of you to be here, you only draw unwanted attention to yourselves.

Jimmy: [*shouts*]: But you promised us that she will be released and you were paid in full!

Vengai: [*to the mob*]: He is right, I am handling this matter. Please move off!

Mrs Bunda: [*points a finger at the interpreter*]: You gave us your word that she will be set free today. We gave you money and yet my daughter is still languishing in prison! You think you can deceive us just like that, I will drag you and your magistrate down ... [*she is pulled away still shouting by Nomsa*].

Interpreter: [*visibly shaken*]: Vengai, my brother, I thought this was a deal between you and me. You have, however, brought to the table a mob that is now baying for my blood.

Vengai: I am very sorry, my brother. These people are just anxious to get this matter done with. So, what is the next step now?

Interpreter: Don't worry; I think the prosecutor is playing a game. If he wanted right away to appeal to the Prosecutor General, he would have straight away informed the court. He has something up his sleeve.

Vengai: You have a point there. My sister's workmates rang me late yesterday saying that a security officer from the bank saw the two of us in the *Beer Engine* yesterday...

Interpreter: [*ashen*]: What! I am finished! [*looks heavenwards*]: Lord, have mercy on me!

Vengai: It is likely that the prosecutor was informed of our meeting yesterday hence his hostile attitude. In light of what we heard in the court just now, we are led to believe that nothing can be salvaged. You and your magistrate have failed and as such, I have been instructed to recover every penny from you.

Interpreter: Don't worry, I will see the magistrate right away and will be back in about 30 minutes. We can turn this thing around.

Vengai: Tell him we want every penny right away. Those people, [*pointing at the mob that was pacing up and down, evidently seething with anger*] won't leave these buildings without all of it today [*exit*].

Interpreter: [*soliloquises as he moves towards the magistrate's office*]. Hey! My ancestral spirits have forsaken me! Only just yesterday they were smiling at me. Maybe, I should have delayed in putting that money I got from this deal down as payment for that house.

In my foolishness, I rang a number of people heralding my prosperity. Even my in-laws were thrilled to hear of my success and now these thieves are demanding their ill-gotten money back. What an embarrassment.

The bank has been struggling to sell houses in that housing scheme. Will the bank refund me before this deal that has gone very wrong explodes in my face today? They may as well argue that a contract came into existence and that I cannot walk away.

This is the end of me. Inevitably, Chikurubi Maximum Security Prison awaits me! Perhaps, it is better to take the rope? But no, this is Harare; things can change in a blink of an eye. Let me see the magistrate. I won't tell him that I was seen at the *Beer Engine* though; lest he abandons me [*he knocks on the magistrate's office door and enters without being invited to do so*].

Magistrate: [*looking up from papers on his desk*]: Mr Interpreter, you have bad news written on your face. Tell me, what is happening out there.

Interpreter: [*collapses on a chair*]: Yes, I bring bad tidings. That thief's relatives and friends nearly attacked me.

Magistrate: Which thief?

Interpreter: Busani, of course.

Magistrate: [*shocked*]: What! What happened?

Interpreter: They said you failed to deliver and they want every penny we took back this very day or else…

Magistrate: Of course, I could have released her as no offence was disclosed by those facts but we need to keep her on a leash. Her trial will soon come up and we will milk them again.

Interpreter: That was a good plan, but the accused person's mother has threatened to drag both of us to the Chief Magistrate. She said she knows people in the high echelons of the police force and politics who will see to it that we rot at the maximum-security prison.

Magistrate: Okay, calm down. I have been thinking of a strategy out of this mess ever since that silly prosecutor threatened to invoke that section.

Interpreter: [*he sits up*]: What is that?

Magistrate: The key lies with the prosecutor. My brethren have in the past told me that he is a player.

Interpreter: So, what is your plan, because I need to give hope to that mob baying for our bloods?

Magistrate: The plan is still hazy, but I need to see Jabu. He can give me advise in this hour of great need.

Interpreter: So?

Magistrate: Go and tell your friend that we are working flat out on this matter. They need not worry. Tell them that this matter is delicate. They have seen how this matter has attracted the attention of all and sundry. The media is awash with the case, so we have to tread very carefully here. I will give you an update before we go into court.

Interpreter: [*stands up*]: No problem boss [*exit*].

Magistrate: [*soliloquises*]: Good Lord! If this case is not handled well, I will be residing at the maximum-security prison by the end this very day. Can you imagine, a magistrate mingling with hard core prisoners in the same prison cell?

But, hang on, I am panicking unnecessarily here. I did not talk to anyone about this deal. They can only cut to pieces he who took their purse. But hang on… from the trend in such cases, the interpreter normally squeals when arrested and the norm is to convict both the magistrate and the interpreter. Even if my case hinges on circumstantial evidence, it just needs the interpreter to mention that I paid for substantial rent arrears, a huge boarding school bill and also that I paid the garage for my car repairs all in one day.

The court will laugh its lungs out considering it is mid-month and most civil servants are dead broke. I have myself convicted fellow civil servants on flimsy evidence. The evidence in my case is overwhelming; I can't let that foolish interpreter mess this one up. [H*e produces a handkerchief and wipes his brow*]: I have to talk to Jabu very urgently. He may give me some valuable advice [*exit*].

Scene V

Opens in the prosecutor's office with the prosecutor and John engaged in a conversation.

Prosecutor: It is obvious that the magistrate has had his share.

John: So, what are you going to do?

Prosecutor: [*smiles*]: It is now our turn to get paid by these thieves.

John: How can that happen?

Prosecutor: I am not going to consult the Prosecutor General over this. Once I do that, this matter will be off our hands. Vultures in that office will drive us off this carcass.

John: So?

Prosecutor: We go back into court and I will say I have failed to speak to the Prosecutor General. But as a sweetener, I will propose the matter be rolled to tomorrow instead of the seven days' time. I can assure you, that by nightfall, we will get irresistible offers from these crooks [*a knock is heard*]: Come in.

Enter the investigating officer

I.O: Hi, Mr Prosecutor. I have just seen the interpreter surrounded by the accused person's relatives and it seems they wanted to tear him apart. I then saw him go upstairs to the magistrate's office with a very forlorn face.

Prosecutor: [*smiles*]: That is not surprising at all.

I.O: Have your spoken to the Prosecutor General?

Prosecutor: The phones are not being picked up, so we will have to roll the matter to tomorrow. But tell me officer, do you really think this accused person can abscond if the right bail conditions are set?

I.O: You know the practice by now Mr Prosecutor. If a lot of money is involved, the officer in charge will invariably oppose the granting of bail notwithstanding that the investigating officer is not opposed to it. I think, if stringent bail conditions are set in this case, we will secure her presence. After all, the whole loot was recovered and even those who were duped are not that enthusiastic in helping with the investigations.

John: Yes, the officer is right. Some of these people are reluctant to come to court lest their business affairs expose them to possible arrests. They are more reluctant if an accused person is being represented by these big city lawyers. You know how these lawyers go out of their way to probe every nook of a business including tough questions on how business people acquired the foreign currency. We might end up with only two or three complainants. The amounts which those complaints lost do not significantly add up to that which was recovered.

Prosecutor: Okay, officer, you can go, and we meet tomorrow at nine. The accused will dine again at the remand prison.

I.O: See you [exit].

Prosecutor: John, there we go my friend! Our main obstacle, the investigating officer, is okay with her being granted bail with tough conditions. As I said, only a foolish prosecutor will ring the Prosecutor General for his opinion!

John: So, what's next?

Prosecutor: Events will happen tonight in Harare once this matter has been postponed to tomorrow.

John: Why are so sure about that?

Prosecutor: [*smiles*]: I have been in this game for too long. This magistrate is still new to the game. Such matters need collaboration. I tell you this very minute, he is consulting his fellow magistrates as regards his precarious position.

John: So, you are the missing cog?

Prosecutor: [*laughs*]: You sum it very well, my dear friend.

John: I need also to play a role. I need to have a serious conversation with her fellow thieves. I will ring you after your court session.

Prosecutor: That is the Harare way, my good friend. See you later.

[*Exit both*].

Scene VI

Opens at a car park outside the court building that same afternoon where the magistrate and Jabu are engaged in a conversation. Smoking a cigarette, the magistrate is pacing up and down.

Magistrate: Thanks, Jabu for coming out here to talk to me.

Jabu: What is it that you could not discuss with me in my office?

Magistrate: It is a grave matter which I could not talk about in the office. You never know who is listening these days.

Jabu: Yes, you are right. Go on then, tell me what is it that is eating you?

Magistrate: My friend, I have a problem in my court. You are aware that my court is handling that bank fraud case which is the talk of the city and media platforms.

Jabu: Yes, I noticed an increased media presence at the courts.

Magistrate: In a nutshell, the accused person's brother approached us and induced us with US$50 000 to grant her bail as the state was opposing bail. The accused person's workmates bankrolled the deal and I granted her bail whereupon the prosecutor jumped up and blocked the grant of bail. He said he wants to seek the Prosecutor General's opinion. He asked me to stand down the matter to give him time to get in touch with his superior. So, as I speak now, he is on the phone.

Jabu: [*laughs*]: He is not going to ring anyone!

Magistrate: This is not a laughing matter, my friend; I need your help.

Jabu: [*patting the magistrate's shoulder*]: He is just showing you that he knows you have been bribed and he wants a share.

Magistrate: Is that so?

Jabu: Yes. I once worked with him and found out quickly that you can't undercut him. If you collaborate with him, you will find that all will end well.

Magistrate: But I have already used the money to pay my bills. Where am I going to get the money to satiate his appetite?

Jabu: Did you say her fellow thieves coughed up the money you received?

Magistrate: Yes.

Jabu: It is not common for friends to pump up that kind of money unless they have an interest in the matter. From past experience, these so-called friends will go all the way and pay for the prosecutor's cut.

Magistrate: You are right. The interpreter from his observations is of the view that the friends are well loaded.

Jabu: I have to go into court now. As I said, have a chat with the prosecutor.

Magistrate: [*throws his cigarette stub away and handshakes with Jabu*]: Thanks, Jabu, I appreciate your guidance.

Jabu: [*smiles*]: You owe me a couple of beers.

Magistrate: [*smiles*]: Once these bad winds pass, it is on me.

[*Exit both*].

Scene VII

Opens in the magistrate's office where the magistrate and the prosecutor are seated and engaged in a conversation.

Magistrate: Thank you for coming, Mr Prosecutor. I had to call you because there is an issue which I greatly need your help with.

Prosecutor: Yes, what is it.

Magistrate: It's a delicate matter which I can't talk about in this office. Can we postpone that Busani Bunda case to tomorrow please?

Prosecutor: No problem.

Magistrate: Can we meet at the *Tipperary's* at 5 o'clock?

Prosecutor: [*smiles*]: I suppose His Worship will be buying drinks?

Magistrate: [*smiles*]: Yes, the drinks are on me.

Prosecutor: [*stands up*]: Okay, see you later [*exit*].

Magistrate: [*soliloquises*]: That prosecutor is a wily fox. I hope he lives up to his reported reputation or else this is the end of me [*he rings the interpreter using his mobile phone*].

Interpreter: [*answers his mobile phone*]: Yes, Your Worship?

Magistrate: I had a word with the prosecutor and I am optimistic that he will play along. We are rolling the matter to tomorrow. Tell your friends that all will end well tomorrow though they have to put together cash for the prosecutor.

Interpreter: [*smiles*]: That is great news, Your Worship. I will right away have a word with them. I will press upon them the dire consequences of their refusal to co-operate.

[***Exit both***].

Scene VIII

Opens at an open space outside the court building where the interpreter is engaged in a conversation with the accused person's relatives.

Interpreter: Okay, guys, I have spoken to the magistrate about your sentiments. He has told me that he is surprised by your attitude. He thought he was dealing with Hararians. I mean, clever people who understand the delicateness of your relative' situation. [*He points a finger at Vengai*]: Did I not tell you that the path you were proposing was a dangerous one when you initially approached me?

Vengai: You did my brother, but some of these people want quick results.

Interpreter: That was a deal between you and me, yet you have gone out to herald this intricate deal to the whole world.

Mrs Bunda: [*contritely*]: We are sorry, my son.

Interpreter: [*to Vengai*]: You said you want your money back? That is not a problem at all; you will get it at the same place tonight. But Busani will go down for a long, long time.

Vengai: [*pleads*]: Please, don't abandon us.

Interpreter: I told the magistrate how you mobbed me, and he is quite annoyed given it is you who approached us. The law will take its course. From the prosecutor's tone, he is going to the wire with this one.

[*He turns to Mrs Bunda*]: Your daughter, Mrs Bunda, will go down for a couple of years. We all know how it is at the maximum-security prison. No food, numerous contagious diseases, such as TB and the deadly Covid-19 virus that recently took down a very big and strong guy. In short, my friends [*he pauses and looks each person present in the eye*], imprisonment in this current climate, means, a quick and inevitable death. Is that want you want in return for some few US dollars, Mrs Bunda?

Mrs Bunda: [*pleadingly*]: No, no, my son, please help us.

Interpreter: Now you are talking like Hararians. The magistrate has told me that he has arranged a rendezvous with the prosecutor to soften his stance on bail after work. So, he is going to postpone this matter to tomorrow instead of the normal seven days as procedurally required by the law of the land. He is definite that she will be released tomorrow.

Vengai: [*turns to his mother*]: That is good news, mum.

Interpreter: So, you have two choices: you can get your money back tonight and Busani stays inside for a couple of years or she is set free tomorrow after just one more night. What will it be my friends? Money back or freedom?

Mrs Bunda: [*to the interpreter*]: My son, money is nothing. What we want is life and that girl in there [she *points at the court building*], I carried her in my womb for nine months. She is very precious to me. She has helped me financially ever since she started working at that bank. Her brother also relies on her, so we can't forsake her for money. Tell the magistrate that we are very grateful for his help.

Interpreter: Vengai, I suppose as a veteran Hararian, you know we have a new entrant to the deal. There is a new dimension to the arrangement.

Vengai: Yes, we have a new player in the form of the prosecutor.

Interpreter: You understand therefore that you will need to bring money for the state.

Vengai: We will definitely get something for the prosecutor.

Interpreter: That will be very resourceful of you, my brother. I like the way you think. If this Harare had more sleek people like you, everyone would prosper. I will meet you at eight tonight at the *Joina City*. Meanwhile, let us go into court.

Vengai: Thank you my brother.

Mrs Bunda: [*to the interpreter*]: Go well my son. You are a true son of the soil; may your ancestral spirits be with you as you execute this delicate matter [*exit the interpreter*].

Vengai [*smiles*]: It is all coming together, mum.

Mrs Bunda: But what about the prosecutor's money? I moved out Busani's money which she had entrusted me with far away as soon as I heard that she had been arrested. I may not get it today to enable you to pay the prosecutor.

Vengai: [*looking surprised*]: So, you spirited some of her money away?

Mrs Bunda: My son, during the reign of Ian Douglas Smith, when this Zimbabwe was still known as Rhodesia, it was common for a suspect's close relatives' houses to be searched for evidence once a suspect had been arrested. We have learnt since then, never to hold evidence in your house and sure enough, the police came after they arrested you and your sister and found nothing in my house.

Vengai: That was very clever of you mum. Leave the money wherever it is. The bank tellers will do anything to spring Busani from prison. So, they will stump up again.

Mrs Bunda: Okay, but be very careful my son. Harare is a slippery place for dealers.

[*Exit both*].

Scene IX

Opens in the court room with the prosecutor addressing the court.

Prosecutor: [*on his feet*]: Your Worship, I gave out earlier on that I wished to get the Prosecutor General's opinion as regards this court's ruling on the issue of bail.

Magistrate: Yes, Mr Prosecutor. What is the position now?

Prosecutor: Well, I have tried to get in touch with my colleagues who handles cases on behalf of the Prosecutor General, but however, it was to no avail.

Magistrate: So, what does the state intend to do?

Prosecutor: Your Worship, I am mindful of the court's ruling. Striking a balance between justice and the freedom of an accused person is always a delicate matter. I am mindful of the accused person's gender, the harsh conditions at the remand prison and in that light; I propose that this matter be rolled to tomorrow instead of the statutory seven days. That way, the accused person will not be greatly prejudiced should the Prosecutor General consent to the granting of bail.

Magistrate: [*a thin smile on his face*]: We are moving towards justice now, Mr Prosecutor. [*To Mr Ndebvu*]: I think, without pre-empting your response Mr Ndebvu, that it is a commendable proposition.

Ndebvu: [*stands up as the prosecutor simultaneously sits down*]. I am grateful, Your Worship, to my learned friend for seeking an early opinion instead of having to wait for seven days. It is natural that I would wish to have my client freed as soon as possible. If the court could bear with me [*he opens up his diary and a moment later, he moves to confer with Busani who is seated in-between prison officers. He moves back to the bar and addresses the magistrate*].

Your Worship, I have explained the position to my client, and she has instructed me to have this bail issue resolved as soon as possible. Having checked my diary, I can avail myself at nine in the morning but will have to leave by eleven in order to attend to another matter in another court. If my learned friend can assure this court that by nine, he will have the Prosecutor General's stance by then, I will be able to attend this court [*he sits down*].

Magistrate: Mr Prosecutor?

Prosecutor: [*stands up*]: I confirm, Your Worship that by nine, I will have the Prosecutor General's decision.

Magistrate: [*writes on papers before him*]: Very well [*to Busani*]: Stand up accused person [*and Busani stands up*]: This matter is rolled to tomorrow for continuation of the bail hearing.

As you have heard, the prosecutor failed to get in touch with the Prosecutor General, but he has promised this court that by nine tomorrow, he will, without fail, furnish this court with his superior's decision. Do you understand?

Busani: Yes, Your Worship.

Magistrate: [*to Busani*]: Stand down [*and Busani sits down*]: Any other business, Mr Prosecutor?

Prosecutor: [*stands up*]: No, Your Worship.

Magistrate: Very well, this court adjourns!

Prosecutor: [*shouts*]: Silence in court! [*all present rise and exchange the customary bows with the magistrate who exits with the interpreter*].

Ndebvu: [*to Vengai who has approached him*]: As you heard, the prosecutor will get back to us by nine tomorrow.

Vengai: [*to Ndebvu*]: What will you do, if he says his boss is of the view that bail should be opposed?

Ndebvu: Don't worry, my friend. You hired the best lawyer in the city. I will take this matter to the highest court on appeal and I will definitely win.

[*Exit all*].

ACT V

Scene I

Opens at Tipperary's pub in the evening that same day with the magistrate having a beer with the prosecutor.

Magistrate: Sorry for messing up your evening, but I have a problem.

Prosecutor: [*smiles*]: Never mind, as long as you are buying the alcohol!

Magistrate: [*smiles*]: I will buy beer till you drop dead drunk tonight.

Prosecutor: It is not often that a magistrate buys a prosecutor beer to that extent.

Magistrate: You are right. The Prosecutor General and Magistrates offices are sworn enemies.

Prosecutor: It's unfortunate that we are ever fighting in our court. Some magistrates and prosecutors form good relationships though.

Magistrate: That is what Jabu told me. He suggested that if I talk to you, we can form a good partnership.

Prosecutor: You mean Jabulani, His Worship?

Magistrate: Yes, a colleague and a good friend of mine.

Prosecutor [*smiles*]: I worked with him for some time in his court and we were quite a team.

Magistrate: He told me that he was disappointed in being moved to another court. He has however managed to set up another partnership in his court.

Prosecutor: [*smiles*]: Jabu is a city guy.

Magistrate: I consulted him today and he said if anyone can fix legal matters, I need not look any further than you. He lauded you as fit for purpose.

Prosecutor: So, what is your problem?

Magistrate: It is that Busani Bunda case. The interpreter took US$50 000 from the brother on condition we granted her bail.

Prosecutor: [*feigning shock*]: Oh!

Magistrate: Unfortunately, you have become an impediment.

Prosecutor: Oh dear, have I?

Magistrate: We should have brought you into the deal, but I needed the money desperately. My landlord wanted to throw me out as I owe him a lot of money. The boarding school also wanted to throw my kids out for non-payment of boarding fees. I had also lately, resorted to jostling with the general public to travel on public transport to work.

Prosecutor: Yes, I have not been seeing your twin cab these days in the parking lot for magistrates. It is unacceptable for a magistrate to travel to work that way.

Magistrate: Well, it was repaired but the garage locked it in for want of payment. So, when the money came my way, I thought I could put it to good use.

Prosecutor: So, how can I help?

Magistrate: Come on now Mr Prosecutor, have you not been listening to what I have been saying? You know what I desperately need.

Prosecutor: Sorry, I don't know what you need.

Magistrate: Okay. May you please withdraw your intention of getting in touch with the Prosecutor General. I have already used their money and if you persist in opposing bail, the next thing is that those thieves will cause a lot of noise leading to my downfall. After all, between you and me, we know that woman is a proper candidate for bail. The bank has a weak case and I doubt if that case can really come up for trial.

Prosecutor: You have a point; it is a weak case and the Prosecutor General will probably laugh in my face for opposing bail. But you guys have benefitted, what about me?

Magistrate: Thank you for understanding my friend. I think we can arrange something. How much do you want?

Prosecutor: I would need to grease the investigating officer and appease the bank security officer who are all hell-bent on having the accused person incarcerated forever.

Magistrate: How much do you want?

Prosecutor: US$300 000 should make us all happy.

Magistrate: I did not get that much myself, but let us do it. I will re-coup my losses in the next games.

Prosecutor: [smiles]: You are a very clever man. I wish we had come to a mutual understanding earlier on. I am, however, going to come on board on one condition.

Magistrate: What is it now, my friend?

Prosecutor: While a charge of fraud with the bank as the complainant will fail to stick, her possession of substantial money found stashed under her bed and that found upon her brother may cause us problems.

Magistrate: You have a point there. Even if we release her on bail, she is likely to fail to convince me that it is her legitimate money. Even a newly appointed magistrate will convict her.

Prosecutor: If we go to trial, she will definitely go to prison. In short, she will come back to haunt us.

Magistrate: So, there is no deal?

Prosecutor: [*laughs*]: Far from that, there is substantial money involved and I am not walking away from it. I propose that once she is granted bail, she leaves the country.

Magistrate: [*pointing a finger at the prosecutor*]: No wonder Jabu said you are the man who can fix problems. By leaving the country, we won't have to deal with her, ever again.

Prosecutor: That is right. If she agrees to leave, then we have a deal, Your Worship.

Magistrate: [*handshakes the prosecutor*]: That should not be a problem, my friend. Let me make some phone calls. Just raise your hand to the barman and beer will be delivered, very swiftly [*exit*].

Prosecutor: [*calls John on his mobile phone*]: There has been a significant development.

John: Really?

Prosecutor: His Worship has confessed to receiving US$50 000 for the purposes of granting bail clandestinely. Having stood in his way, he wants me to stop getting in touch with the Prosecutor General. He has accepted my fee of US$300 000. He is, I believe, talking to his associate now.

John: [*excitedly*]: Good stuff. I told you these thieves stole millions.

Prosecutor: I told him however that the deal is dependent upon one condition.

John: What condition?

Prosecutor: That Busani leaves the country tomorrow because even if we release her on bail, she will still have to present herself for the trial. Given the evidence against her, she is unlikely to escape a conviction of being found in possession of property and failing to account for it.

John: Yes, the evidence against her is insurmountable.

Prosecutor: His Worship is on the phone presumably to the interpreter to convey my demand. I will keep you posted [*he cuts John off as the magistrate enters*].

Magistrate: [*to the prosecutor*]: I have spoken to the interpreter who is at the *Joina City* in the company of the bank tellers about your request. I have also asked him to convey in a very grave tone of Busani's assured short term freedom if she hangs around after being granted bail. We will hear from them soon.

Prosecutor: [*laughs*]: I like the way that interpreter uses language to scare people in court.

Magistrate: Yes, he is very effective. Let's drink to prosperity!

Prosecutor: [*clink glasses*]: Cheers!

Magistrate: Cheers! I think we will make a formidable team.

Prosecutor: [*raises his glass*]: A toast to our new partnership!

Magistrate: [*raises his glass*]: To a new partnership! [*they both drink from their glasses*].

[*Exit both after exchanging mobile phone numbers*].

Scene II

Takes place that same night at the Joina City where the interpreter, Vengai and the bank tellers are imbibing alcohol. The scene opens with the interpreter hanging up his phone.

Interpreter: [*smiles*]: I am the bearer of very good news my dear friends. I have just been speaking to the man who rules our court [*he gulps his beer*].

Tom: You mean the magistrate?

Interpreter: [*burps*]: Yes, the man himself [*he picks up his beer and takes a swig*].

Vengai: [*impatiently*]: Go on, tell us the good news.

Interpreter: The prosecutor has changed his mind. He is not going to communicate with the Prosecutor General. So, your friend will be released tomorrow.

Nomsa: Hurray!

Jimmy: Good news indeed and what is the bad news?

Interpreter: Nothing that you guys can't handle. The prosecutor needs just US$350 000 to execute the deal and all your troubles will just vanish.

Tom: [*aghast*]. US$350 000! [*points a finger at the interpreter*]: You guys, what do you take us for? Millionaires?

Interpreter: Sorry guys, I am just the bearer of news.

Tom: We have paid through the nose already and we are yet to see any fruit.

Jimmy: Is the sum negotiable?

Interpreter: I am afraid it is not negotiable. The prosecutor having publicly said he was aggrieved by the magistrate' decision will have a lot of explaining to do tomorrow when it turns out that he has changed his mind overnight. Definitely, a number of people will want to know what softened him.

Tom: So that justifies this colossal sum?

Interpreter: If you have lived in this city for a long time, you will have heard of prosecutors who went to prison for less serious deeds. If they throw him out of work, he will need something to fall back on. If there is no such safety net, why should he put his neck on the line? Tell me, why he should accept peanuts from strangers and risk his neck? You guys are a joke [*he starts to dial on his mobile*]: I will ring them now and convey your decision.

Jimmy: [*to the interpreter*]: Wait. Don't call them yet.

Interpreter: [*sneers*]: You lot, you think you are the only ones who want to make money in Harare?

Nomsa: Calm down guys [*to the interpreter*]: Did you say all our problems will disappear just like that?

Interpreter: Indeed, as aptly sung by Winky D, that Zimbabwe dancehall artist, all your problems will disappear. The prosecutor will work with the police and your people at the bank and all the potential cases against all of you will be dropped for lack of evidence.

Jimmy: Are you sure about this?

Interpreter: I swear.

Nomsa: [*to the interpreter*]: Could you excuse us for a minute?

Interpreter: Before I go, I have also been told that the prosecutor as part of the deal would want Busani to leave the country tomorrow.

Jimmy: Why is that?

Interpreter: He said even if she is granted bail, the evidence against her is very strong and she will invariably be convicted for possession of money found on her. In short, her liberty will be a temporary one as she will have to be sent to prison.

Nomsa: But, can't they not find a loophole to find her not guilty. She has funds stashed away to pay for that and we can also chip in.

Interpreter: [*scoffs*]: My sister, any newly qualified prosecutor would relish to handle such an easy case. What about our seasoned prosecutor whom I have witnessed cross-examining hard-core criminals till they broke down? Busani's case would be like a hot knife cutting through butter. We would have helped her immensely up to the end of this first round.

I can assure you, that if she hangs around for round two, that is the trial stage, she will be floored in no time and never rise again. It's suicidal, take heed. If I were her...

Jimmy: [*interrupts the interpreter*]: Okay, I think you have made your point. We need to discuss this among ourselves. Give us a few minutes.

Interpreter: [*stands up*]: You will find me at the bar [*he soliloquises as moves away*]: There is need for me to employ subterfuge here. If I tell them that the money is for this pending case only, they will refuse to pay.

I will utilise any means to keep the house I bought with their money. Didn't that popular blind singer Paul Matavire sing his lungs out, that fortune knocks at a man's door once in a lifetime? Well, fortunate has done that, this is my turn [*exit*].

Tom: If paying solves all our problems, I say let's pay up. We have a lot to lose if this matter explodes. I think the prosecutor is also very wise in suggesting that Busani should disappear into thin air.

Nomsa: I agree. Hanging around won't help her or any of us.

Jimmy: It is a good idea. All of us have been the USA, UK and other First World countries and have even toyed with the idea of living there for good. Busani and I still have valid visas to one or two countries, hence leaving this sorry country will not be a problem. Let's pay up.

Nomsa: Let's share the bill.

Tom: But should Busani not contribute also?

Jimmy: Come on now, Tom. We can't even reach her. She will repay us once she is liberated.

Nomsa: Jimmy is right. What are friends for anywhere?

Tom: Okay. But I would like to hear it from the horse's mouth. I don't trust that interpreter.

Nomsa: Me too. He is a sly one [*she beckons the interpreter to come to them*].

Tom: [*to the interpreter*]: The deal is on. The money is a stone throw away.

Interpreter: [*smiles*]: That is very good for your cause.

Jimmy: However, we want to hear from the prosecutor himself before we hand over the money tonight.

Interpreter: That can be arranged. Excuse me [*he moves away from the group and calls the magistrate using his mobile phone*]. Hi, boss.

Magistrate: What is the position my good friend?

Interpreter: They have the money stashed nearby. They also understand that the accused person has to leave Zimbabwe tomorrow.

Magistrate: That is very good.

Interpreter: They, however want to talk to the prosecutor before the money is handed over. They need assurance that they won't be further hiccups.

Magistrate: The prosecutor is with me right now, hold on [*he turns to the prosecutor*]: It is in the bag my friend. But they just want to meet you and get assurance that all will end well tomorrow.

Prosecutor: [*to the magistrate*]: That is a small matter. I will handle that. They will have to come here for obvious reasons.

Magistrate [*to the prosecutor*]: Yes, it has to appear as if it is them who joins us in case, we have some foolish policemen setting up a trap.

Prosecutor: [*to the magistrate*]: That is not the way it works my friend. You will have to go before they get here. It is unwise for a magistrate to be seen in the company of an accused person's relatives or friends.

Magistrate: [*looking very relieved*]: That is good thinking, my friend.

Prosecutor: However, I will not collect any money from them tonight; the interpreter will bring it to another rendezvous.

Magistrate: Okay [*he rings the interpreter who answers his mobile phone*]: The prosecutor is waiting for all of you here, but he will not receive the money from them. Do as usual and get in touch with me later on. I am leaving now.

Interpreter: [*on his phone*]: No problem, Your Worship.

Magistrate: [*hangs his phone up and speaks to the prosecutor*]: They are coming. See you later [*exit*].

Prosecutor: [*soliloquises*]: This is turning out very well for me. All that US$300 000 for me? It would have taken me ages to earn that kind of money on the straight and narrow. Indeed, God is great [*exit*].

Interpreter: [*to the bank tellers*]: The prosecutor wants us to meet him at the *Tipperary's*. You will hand the money to me. He will just talk to you.

Jimmy: [*smiles*]: Nomsa, the queen of cash! Please go and bring the cash.

Nomsa: No problem [*exit*].

Interpreter: How long will she take?

Tom: [*to the interpreter*]: We are bank tellers; we can have any amount of cash as and when we want. The money is readily stashed nearby.

Interpreter: How nice.

Jimmy: Let's drink up guys. We need to wrap this up tonight. Tomorrow we will paint Harare red with the prisoner! I miss her so much!

Tom: [*raises his glass*]: To freedom!

Jimmy: [*raises his glass also*]: To freedom!

[*Exit all*].

Scene III

Opens thirty minutes later with the bank tellers, Vengai and the interpreter joining the prosecutor at the Tipperary's. Tom attempts to handshake the prosecutor.

Prosecutor: [*he declines the handshake*]: In our world, we don't shake hands with accused person's friends and potential arrestees. This is a public place; the world is watching.

Tom: Sorry, Mr prosecutor, I didn't know.

Prosecutor: No problem. Let's get to business, shall we?

Nomsa: Yes. You are the only person in that court who is opposing bail but we understand you have changed your mind.

Prosecutor: Yes.

Tom: So, what is going to happen tomorrow?

Prosecutor: She gets out. You are aware that it was proposed by her lawyer that she will surrender her passport as part of her bail conditions.

Vengai: Yes.

Prosecutor: You also understand that it is in her interest to leave the country tomorrow for some time.

Jimmy: Yes. But what about us?

Prosecutor: I don't understand what you are saying.

Tom: The interpreter said you were going to drop her case and kill off all potential cases against us.

Prosecutor: [*smiles*]: Not so fast my friends. The interpreter is a lay person and he erred to suggest that the slate will be wiped clean by this payment. Forgive him for his enthusiasm.

Tom: So, what are you saying?

Prosecutor: I am not going to lie to you guys. We are working in partnership now. Investigations are in their infancy and cases might arise against you. If that happens, I will use my clout to keep you out of prison.

Jimmy: Thank you, Mr Prosecutor.

Prosecutor: However, the accused person's continued presence in this country poses very grave danger to anyone assisting her to evade justice. Do you understand?

Tom: Yes, I think it would be naive on our part to think that with a magic wand, this matter will be erased without people raising eyebrows.

Prosecutor: Good. She has to leave the country tomorrow. I believe you can for a small fee make arrangements for a passport for her. If not, I have sources that can do it for her, first thing in the morning.

Nomsa: No problem, we have contacts at the Registrar General's office.

Prosecutor: Very good. Make sure you book a flight for her to leave tomorrow [*stands up*]: I will see you tomorrow [*exit*].

Vengai: [*aside*]: Oh, my God. This is all my fault. Now she has to take flight. How will mum take it?

Jimmy: I may equally have to leave the country my friends.

Nomsa: I have to go guys; I have to see some people as regards that passport and negative Covid-19 tests as she won't fly out without such results.

Tom: At this late hour?

Nomsa: [*laughs*]: Have you forgotten the meaning of Harare? It means a city whose people never sleep [*exit*].

Jimmy: [*to the interpreter*]: My friend, I think it's all in there [*he pushes a satchel to the interpreter*].

Interpreter: [*moves quickly away from the satchel*]: I am not touching that thing in here. Take it outside and give it to a guy in a yellow Nissan Micra which is parked just at the entrance. He will also be donning a yellow t-shirt.

Jimmy: No problem [*exits the bar with the satchel*].

Vengai: Thank you, guys, for rescuing my sister. I have to go and inform my mum of this latest development. [*To the interpreter*]: I will see you tomorrow [*exit*].

Interpreter: [*as Jimmy re-enters the bar minus the satchel, he stands up*]: I will see you guys tomorrow [*exit*].

Jimmy: See you my brother and thanks a million.

Tom: I hope this is the end of Busani's woes.

Jimmy: I hope so.

[*Exit all*].

Scene IV

Opens in the magistrate's lounge and present is the magistrate and the court interpreter.

Magistrate: [*receiving the US dollars*]: Well, well, you have delivered again Mr Interpreter.

Interpreter: Always at your service, Your Worship!

Magistrate: How much do we have here?

Interpreter: $350 000 as demanded by the prosecutor.

Magistrate: A pity we got less, but I tell you, things will run smoothly from now given that we will be working in cahoots with the state counsel.

Interpreter: [*smiles*]: Roping in the prosecutor is the greatest coup to our enterprise.

Magistrate: I foresee greater and bigger things ahead, my friend.

Interpreter: [*smiles*]: It can only get better, Your Worship.

Magistrate: [*stands up and grabs a bottle of whiskey*]: A special occasion like this deserves downing good waters my friend [*he pours 4 torts per glass and hands one to his associate*].

Interpreter: Indeed, Your Worship! Thanks!

Magistrate: Cheers! I will ring the prosecutor to come and collect his loot. At least we can sleep well tonight, my friend.

Interpreter: I have been imagining myself as a resident of that dreaded Chikurubi Maximum Security Prison all day.

Magistrate: [*chuckles*]: Fear had also engulfed me!

Interpreter: You know how inmates are attracted to light skinned men in prison just as a moth is attracted to the light.

Magistrate: [*laughs*]: I know!

Interpreter: Given my light skin, I would rather kill myself before those uncouth men lay their rough hands on me [*he clicks his fingers*]: God forbid!

Magistrate: [*laughs*]: The horrendous scenes we see during our prison visits haunt me every day. I keep seeing images of prisoners with ribs sticking out due to starvation, prisoners walking about, literally naked, the stench itself is so overpowering that it puts me off food for days. I can't imagine myself living within that population.

Interpreter: A prison officer told me of an upsurge in deaths due to the Covid-19 virus in that prison. In addition, he said, if you don't have relatives who can bring you meals, your days on earth, unfortunately, will be reduced greatly.

Magistrate: In this current climate of severe economic meltdown, who would perpetually feed you for years? Factor in the current Covid 19 pandemic. Who would be brave to play hide and seek games with the police and soldiers who are enforcing the lockdown rules in order to bring food to a prisoner? We have heard rumours of the endgame of such encounters: a few broken bones, my friend.

Interpreter: In just a few weeks, if not a few days, your sympathisers will lose heart and abandon you.

Magistrate: My main fear was meeting those criminals I sent to prison.

Interpreter: [*chuckles*]: Indeed, they will have a field day if you were to land there.

Magistrate: We are the most hated judicial officers. Even those who knew that invariably they had to go to prison, will gleefully lay their hands on me.

Interpreter: But will the prison officers not sort of give you a safe cell, far from the madding crowd.

Magistrate: [*laughs*]: Forget William Shakespeare my friend, without my robes, I will have been debased to a common criminal!

Interpreter: [*finishes drinking his whiskey and stands up*]: This near mishap is bone chilling. I have to go; the courier is waiting for me outside.

Magistrate: [*laughs*]: Yes, the courier is an apt title for your cousin. I hope you treated him well from your cut.

Interpreter: [*laughs*]: Ever since he got retrenched and joined our enterprise, he has grown fatter!

Magistrate: [*stands up*]: I will see you tomorrow. Take care.

Interpreter: No problem boss [*exit*].

Magistrate: [*soliloquises*]: This is why I like Harare. If you use your brains, there is no need to trek abroad. The pastures are ever green here. Let me spirit away my cut before the prosecutor turns up [*he counts out US$50 000 and hides it beneath a sofa and rings the prosecutor*].

Prosecutor: [*answers his mobile*]. His Worship, how are you doing?

Magistrate: Your stuff is here.

Prosecutor: That was quickly executed.

Magistrate: In light of our mission scheduled for tomorrow morning, I suppose it is ideal that you pick up the goods tonight.

Prosecutor: You are quite right. Where shall we meet?

Magistrate: Can you come to my house, number 19 James Court?

Prosecutor: I know the place. I will see you shortly [*he hangs up and exit*].

Magistrate: [*soliloquises*]: It is worrying that he even knows where I stay. This prosecutor is notorious for coming to court late. Funny enough, he won't be late in picking up money! This world!

But on another note, his coming on board could be that elusive Holy Grail. Fellow magistrates have told me of their golden harvests emanating from working in cahoots with their prosecutors. This is it then!

[Exit].

Scene V

Opens at Mrs Bunda's house where she is engaged in a conversation with her son, Vengai.

Mrs Bunda: So, this prosecutor said my daughter has to skip the country?

Vengai: Yes, he says it is better that way, for now.

Mrs Bunda: Did he say when will she be able to come back home?

Vengai: No time frame was set. They say if you run away for twenty years, you won't be prosecuted upon return.

Mrs Bunda: [*aghast*]: Twenty years! I will have turned in my grave many times. Are you sure?

Vengai: A friend of mine who is a lawyer said that.

Mrs Bunda: [*contemptuously*]: You are seriously saying a criminal can flee abroad, evade capture for twenty years and then simply stroll back into the country and all is forgiven? Given that the lawyer is your friend, he was likely to have been very drunk just as you were when he uttered that rubbish.

Vengai: He wasn't drunk.

Mrs Bunda: Anyway, what do you think is the best for your sister given that you are now the head of this family?

Vengai: She has been of late talking about leaving the country anyway. It might be for the best.

Mrs Bunda: Yes, for both of them.

Vengai: Who is the other one?

Mrs Bunda: She told me that Jimmy, her workmate, wants to marry her. They had planned to move to the United States after their wedding.

105

Vengai: [*surprised*]: What! Jimmy marrying Busani?

Mrs Bunda: Since your father passed away, you now act on his behalf and as per our custom, you are not supposed to be privy to those proceedings until you are formally informed.

Vengai: Now that you have told me, I suppose Jimmy has to marry her before she goes.

Mrs Bunda: [*laughs*]: My son, even a thief hiding behind a bush will come out and laugh at your extreme greediness. You are always thinking of receiving money!

Vengai: [*dismissively*]: It is our culture mum. Co-habiting is frowned upon; hence honourable men pay their dues to their in-laws.

Mrs Bunda: Jimmy comes from a well cultured family. He will do the right thing.

Vengai: I am keeping a close eye on him from henceforth. Any cultural transgression by him, will result in the payment of hefty charges.

Mrs Bunda: Forget about Jimmy for now; let us talk about your sister.

Vengai: I suppose the idea of her leaving the country is hurting you so much?

Mrs Bunda: Yes, it pains. It is too soon.

Vengai: You will need to take extra care then of your poor health and that leaves me to take care of her businesses.

Mrs Bunda: [*snarls*]: Given your propensity for throwing money away, I won't let you near her properties and businesses.

Vengai: Mum, do not worry. I have the business acumen; it is only that my deals of late went awry.

Mrs Bunda: Business acumen, my foot! If it were not for your posturing like a peacock with her money, she would be asleep now in her silken sheets! Over my dead body will you lay your hands on her properties and money!

Vengai: Calm down, mum. Anyway, we need to surrender her passport at the clerk of court as part of the bail conditions. Do you know where it is?

Mrs Bunda: She left it here when she moved out to her new property. But how will she fly out without it?

Vengai: Her friend Nomsa has friends at the passport office who will facilitate a new one before noon tomorrow.

Mrs Bunda: That Nomsa is a very clever girl. If I had a worthy son, I would move mountains to have her as my daughter-in-law.

Vengai: I am your only son, are you suggesting that I not worthy of her?

Mrs Bunda: [*chuckles*]: Vengai, my son, she is out of your league!

Vengai: If I had money, she would fall for me.

Mrs Bunda: [*laughs*]: She has her own money, what she needs is a man who can match her intellect.

Vengai: [*laughs*]: She is just a common thief. There are no more brains in her than a monkey.

Mrs Bunda: Busani told me she has a degree in something to do with banking from overseas.

Vengai: [*sneers*]: Any fool with money can buy a degree from overseas these days. In the city, there is talk of a famous man who bought a doctorate degree from overseas and is now calling himself a doctor! Anyway, let us talk about your daughter, not that clever for nothing Nomsa.

Mrs Bunda: Very well. Does Busani know she has to jet out of the country tomorrow?

Vengai: I spoke to her lawyer about the whole arrangement and he said he will convey the message to her.

Mrs Bunda: I will miss her so much and I hope Jimmy will go with her.

Vengai: [*chuckles*]: Don't worry mum, she is not the only child.

Mrs Bunda: [*jovially pushes him away*]: Get away from my sight!

[*Exit both*].

Scene VI

Opens in the magistrate's lounge late that same night with the magistrate and the prosecutor engaged in a conversation over a bottle of whiskey.

Prosecutor: You have an expensive taste my friend!

Magistrate: [*chuckles*]: A toast, my friend! Cheers! [*they clink glasses*].

Prosecutor: [*salivating at the bundles of US dollars on the table*]: Is that it?

Magistrate: Yes, it is all there [*he deposits the money into a satchel*].

Prosecutor: [*smiles*]: I will take your word [*he receives the satchel and moves towards the exit*].

Magistrate: How did it go with the bankers?

Prosecutor: [*stands by the doorway*]: The bank tellers understood that their friend will have to scamper as soon as she regains her freedom tomorrow.

Magistrate: Good advice, for it is unlikely that she can just keep that money.

Prosecutor: Having taken their money, it would put us in a very invidious position to have to send her back to prison.

Magistrate: Anyway, granting her bail is like opening a bird's cage. Common sense will tell it to fly away.

Prosecutor: [*laughs*]: Okay, see you tomorrow, my friend [*he exits*].

Magistrate: [*he goes into his bedroom and he is surprised to find his wife still awake*]: I thought you were fast asleep, my dear.

Martha: Don't dear me! Who was that man I heard you talking to at this late hour?

Magistrate: Just a prosecutor who prosecutes in my court.

Martha: There has been unusual late-night visits lately from people from your workplace. Is your court now sitting after hours in my house?

Magistrate: [*laughs*]: Harare does not sleep, my dear [*sitting on the bed next to her*].

Martha: [*she moves away from him*]: I am very worried. Whenever that foxy interpreter comes to my home, I see you thereafter splashing out money.

Magistrate: Never mind that young man.

Martha: We had rent arrears, but surprisingly, the landlord and his wife merrily waved at me today, whereas ordinarily, they would have stopped me for a chat about it. What is going on, my husband?

Magistrate: [*laughs*]: As the man of the house, I sorted out the problem.

Martha: I also sought to negotiate for more time to pay the boarding school fees, but the school clerk over the phone told me you had cleared the debt today. I notice also that you managed to extricate your twin cab from the garage having failed do so due to lack of money [*she puts her hand on his shoulder*]: My dear, each time the interpreter comes, money follows him into this house.

My dear, are you back to your old, nefarious deeds? We have quarrelled many times in the past over bribes and corruption which obviously is an environment you thrive in.

Magistrate: Don't worry, there are no deals involved. It is a legitimate business.

Martha: What business do you do, which, me, your wife does not know about?

Magistrate: Look, an astute businessperson only heralds his enterprise when it bears fruit. Mine has borne fruit. Here, get yourself something… [*he produces a bundle of US dollars from his pocket and tries to hand it to her*].

Martha: [*she declines to take the money*]: I eat what I earn, keep your ill-gotten money.

Magistrate: [*laughs*]: This is Harare my dear, you need to shake off that virtuous rural mentality. It is dog eat dog in Harare. Your academic degree won't feed you in this city. I have a busy day tomorrow, good night.

Martha: [*sighs*]: It is just a matter of time before they nab you and throw you in prison. Why can't you live within your means?

Magistrate: [*laughs*]: This is Harare my dear, you snooze, you lose!

Martha: I do not relish being a single parent. Are you not ashamed of yourself? Even if you don't have any conscience, very soon, they will cart you to prison where you will die from diseases or get killed by those you imprisoned falsely because they could not afford to bribe you [*she pokes him in the face*]. Mark my words, you corrupt man!

Magistrate: [*smiles*]: You worry unnecessarily, my dear wife.

Martha: One of these days, the wheels will come off, mark my words.

[*Exit both*].

ACT VI

Scene I

Opens the next day at the Harare magistrates court in the morning and Mr Ndebvu is having a private word in the holding cells with Busani who is clad in a yellow prison dress.

Mr Ndebvu: Hi. Cheer up. Today is the day you will leave the dungeons.

Busani: [*warming up*]: Really? What is happening?

Mr Ndebvu: Your brother and your workmates worked really hard and managed to persuade the prosecutor to let you out on bail.

Busani: How did they do that?

Mr Ndebvu: I am not privy to what happened, but I suppose there were some unethical actions involved. I have, however, been instructed to convey a message to you.

Busani: What is that?

Mr Ndebvu: After you are granted bail, you are to leave the country today.

Busani: What! Why?

Mr Ndebvu: I am informed that your associates have been told that you are likely to be convicted if you wait for the trial.

Busani: As my lawyer, what are my chances if I stay put and face the trial?

Mr Ndebvu: I will not adopt the attitude of a lawyer who is struggling to make ends meet in response your question. A hungry lawyer, if asked by a client about their prospects of success at an upcoming trial, will vehemently tell the client amidst great posturing that they will be victorious. Obviously, if the lawyer says there are no prospects of success, the client will simply cross the street and engage a lawyer that will exuberantly guarantee victory.

The desire is to make money, but I have made legitimate money and I will answer your question truthfully. That prosecutor is a crafty one; he will dutifully read all relevant statutes and will definitely come up with some charge against you. I do not fully know the evidence that the state has against you, but it is unlikely that your conduct could escape the loosely crafted statutes.

You may get fined, but given the sum involved, it could land you in jail. Of course, I will fight in your corner. I however, suggest that you take their advice and hastily put distance between yourself and this country.

Busani: But how can I leave the country without a passport?

Mr Ndebvu: Another passport in your names will be ready today.

Busani: How will they get another passport for me?

Mr Ndebvu: [*smiles*]: It seems the clerk of court does not inform the Registrar General's office speedily enough about passports being held at court. Therefore, anyone with the right connections can obtain another passport before alarm is raised. I hear it happens, but as I said, I am not privy to the circumstances. Do you understand?

Busani: [*smiles*]: That is great deception.

Mr Ndebvu: Harare, my dear, is a city of deceit. Anyway, they want a reply. Do you wish to leave the country today?

Busani: But where to?

Mr Ndebvu: I don't know.

Busani: Thank you. Tell them I am ready to leave tonight as long as Jimmy is coming.

Mr Ndebvu: Your mother told me just now that your fiancé wants to leave with you tonight. As soon as I convey your response, he will buy first class tickets, whatever the cost. He is not at court this morning but in the city, making arrangements for both of you. This is a top secret; do not utter any of what I said to you to anyone. Whatever the court officials will say in court today, would be the execution of their plan. Do not question anything, just follow the script. I will meet you in court shortly [*exit*].

Busani: [*soliloquising*]: Being jailed has stressed me so much [*she looks heavenwards*]: Thank you, dear Jesus, for coming to my aid and I will praise you every day of my life. Oh, thank you Lord! A prison officer told me that my case is trending on Facebook, Twitter and Instagram let alone on WhatsApp. To think that I was brought up in a Christian family, attending church every Sunday and then it comes to this. This is very embarrassing. I, therefore need to leave this horrid city and start a new life without being called a fraudster on the streets by all and sundry [*exit*].

Scene II

Opens in the prosecutor's office, where the prosecutor is engaged in a conversation with John.

Prosecutor: I managed to get the US$300 000 and it is stashed away safely. The thieving bank tellers also agreed that Busani leaves the country today.

John: That is good news. Have they sorted the travelling documents?

Prosecutor: They said that is not a problem.

John: Good, because I do not want to get involved in their escape bid. It might complicate issues.

Prosecutor: Quite right. A menacing outlook on your part is essential in inspiring fear into them. These people have more money than we think.

John: Money is not a problem to those thieves, my friend [*they high five*].

Prosecutor: I am not however convinced that all this wealth came from the bank tellers merely duping bank clients as the bank alleges.

John: You are right. The bank has sent one of our executive officers, Mr Dehwa, to South Africa as we don't know precisely the magnitude of the fraud. An internal audit will not suffice given the corruption within the bank. So, Mr Dehwa has been consulting a high-profile audit firm in South Africa and their team will be in Harare very soon.

Prosecutor: I think we have merely scratched the surface here. We need to move fast and mop up that money out there before the bank recovers it.

John: You have a point, my friend. There is need for speed.

Prosecutor: Yes, faster than those actors in the *Fast and Furious* movies. You need to arrest one of them on flimsy evidence and charge him or her with the same allegations. We will then release that person on a point of law using the views expressed in Busani's case by His Worship.

John: Yes, but this time, we will share the proceeds.

Prosecutor: No problem at all.

John: I think if we cause the arrest of a woman, the thieves will rally to her cause quicker than if a man is arrested.

Prosecutor: Quite right, my friend. When a woman is nabbed, people normally rush to extricate her from the dungeons!

John: That is why I like you, my dear friend. I will inform the investigating officer to arrest Nomsa as soon as Busani flies out tonight.

Prosecutor: She is a very good candidate, my friend. Splendid! [*a knock is heard, and he shouts*]: Enter!

Enter the investigating officer

I. O: Good morning, gentlemen.

Prosecutor: Good morning, officer.

John: Morning officer.

Prosecutor: [*to the investigating officer*]: We have just been discussing with John that the fraudulent activities at the bank should be treated with the utmost seriousness they deserve.

I. O: There is a lot of paperwork which I need to go through to enable me to come up with charges that will stand in court.

Prosecutor: Millions could have been stolen for all we know but you have just arrested one person only. That does not augur well with the seriousness which should be accorded to this grand fraud. We need the suspects to be placed on remand such that the court has control over their movements. Any one of them can run away now and there is nothing we can do about it.

I.O: I haven't been idle Mr Prosecutor. In fact, I have prepared court papers for Jimmy Moyo. I understand he will be coming to court today, so I will lie in wait for him.

John: [*smiles*]: That is great detective work, officer.

I.O: [*leaving the office*]: Let me look around for him. Upon sight I will immediately spring on him [*exit*].

Prosecutor: There comes another client my friend! [*they high five*].

John: But will these bank tellers not say they have paid enough?

Prosecutor: No, they can't say that. The money was not for a blanket stoppage on the police doing further investigations into the fraudulent activities at the bank. We will deal with each case on an individual basis.

John: Quite right. It is the prerogative of the police to arrest any suspect. Their ill-gotten wealth will be ours!

Prosecutor: Well summed up, my friend. Let us proceed to court.

[Exit both].

Scene III

Opens in the court room and it is the matter of the State versus Busani Bunda being heard. The magistrate is addressing the prosecutor who is standing at the bar.

Magistrate: Mr Prosecutor, you asked for a deferment of this matter yesterday, it being your intention of getting advice from the Prosecutor General.

Prosecutor: Yes, Your Worship.

Magistrate: What is the position now?

Prosecutor: Your Worship, having had further time to digest the court's ruling, the state no longer opposes the granting of bail. This is based upon having had the occasion to speak at length with the investigating officer. He told me that given that all was recovered, it would be unjust to lock the accused person away... [*there is clapping and ululation in the gallery*].

Court Orderly: [*shouts*]: Silence in court!

Magistrate: Thank you, Mr Prosecutor [*he writes on papers before him*]: Mr Ndebvu, do you wish to say anything?

Ndebvu: [*stands up and simultaneously, the prosecutor sits down*]: I must commend my learned friend here for rightfully conceding that the accused person is a right candidate to be granted bail. Given my learned friend has not suggested any sum bail or other bail conditions, the defence proposes that the court adopts that which I proposed yesterday.

Magistrate: Mr Prosecutor, what do you say to the defence's suggestion? [*Mr Ndebvu sits down as the prosecutor stands up*].

Prosecutor: Your Worship, the state agrees with the sum and conditions proposed by the defence [*he sits down*].

Magistrate: [*shuffles papers before him and addresses Busani*]: Stand up accused person and listen very carefully.

Busani [*stands up in the dock between two prison officers*]: Yes, Your Worship.

Magistrate: You have heard yourself that the state is no longer opposed to the granting of bail. You are therefore released on bail in the sum $10 000 bond notes. You are also to surrender your passport to the clerk of court.

Further, you must also report to the CID Fraud Squad thrice a week between 9: 00 a.m. and 5:00 p.m. on Mondays, Wednesdays and Fridays. You must also reside at your given address until this matter is finalised. Do you understand?

Busani: [*smiles*]: Yes, Your Worship.

Magistrate: You have seen how tough life is in prison and the dangers posed by the Covid-19 pandemic to inmates. So, make sure you avail yourself on your next remand date. Also make sure you report as stipulated. If you breach these conditions, we will lock you up. Your lawyer will explain all this to you if you don't understand what I have said. Sit down.

Busani: I understand [*she sits down*].

Ndebvu: [*stands up*]: I am obliged, Your Worship [*he sits down*].

Magistrate: Mr Prosecutor may you agree on the next remand date with the defence counsel.

Prosecutor: [*confers with Mr Ndebvu and stands up*]: My learned friend has indicated that they can pay and also surrender the passport today. Therefore, we have agreed with my learned friend that the accused person be remanded to 28 May, Your Worship [*he sits down*].

Mr Ndebvu: [*stands up*]: The date is by consent, Your Worship [*he sits down*].

Magistrate: [*to Busani*]: Stand up accused person [*Busani stands up*]. Be at this court by 9 in the morning on 28 May, this year and not next year without fail [*gallery laughs*].

Busani: Yes, Your Worship.

Magistrate: [*to Busani*]: Very well, stand down [*Busani smiles and waves to people in the gallery and is led away into a side door by prison officers*].

Prosecutor: [*stands up*]: I have no further business, Your Worship.

Magistrate: [*picks up papers before him and shouts as he rises*]: This court adjourns!

Prosecutor: [*standing up*]: Silence in court! [*exit the magistrate and the interpreter and Busani's relatives and friends mob Mr Ndebvu at the bar*].

Mrs Bunda: [*handshakes the lawyer*]: Well done, Sir [*she then dances and people around her laugh*].

Mr Ndebvu: [*to Mrs Bunda*]: You are welcome, madam.

Court Orderly: [*jokingly to Mrs Bunda*]: I hope you are not going to faint again madam [*people around her laugh*].

Mrs Bunda: [*smiles*]: No! Never again, my son! This whole matter is over.

Vengai: [*as the prosecutor walks out of the court*]: Thank you, Mr Prosecutor.

Prosecutor: [*smiles*]: We are not hard-hearted, Mr Bunda. In fact, we are soft as wool [*he exits carrying his files*].

Vengai: [*to Mr Ndebvu*]: Did you manage to convey my message to my sister?

Mr Ndebvu: Yes, she said that is not a problem at all [*he puts a file in his briefcase and shuts it*]: I have to go now. Follow the Court Orderly to the clerk of court's office and surrender Busani's passport and also pay the required money for bail.

Vengai: Thank you. I will pick her up from the remand prison.

[*Exit all*].

Scene IV

Opens in the afternoon at Mrs Bunda's house where after Busani's release from prison, her friends and relatives are celebrating her release.

Mrs Bunda: [*whispering to Busani*]: Make sure you don't tell everyone that you will be leaving the country today.

Busani: Mum, this is the umpteenth time you have said this. All those who are here are my friends. No one will stab me in the back.

Mrs Bunda: I know Harare better than you when it comes to backstabbers. Is everything ready?

Busani: Yes, Nomsa brought me my new passport.

Mrs Bunda: She is a very resourceful young woman. How I wish your brother could marry her.

Busani: [*laughs*]: Ha! Ha! She is beyond the reach of that useless son of yours!

Mrs Bunda: Don't call him useless, he ran around risking his own neck for your release.

Busani: [*bitterly*]: Mum, have you just forgotten that he caused my incarceration? I will never forgive him. To steal my money and then dole it to the whole of Harare by buying alcohol is unforgivable.

Mrs Bunda: [*holding Busani's hands*]: My daughter, I know you have previously given him money to start numerous businesses and nothing came out of them. You are a generous person. God will give you more. Please forgive him.

Busani: What he did pains me very much, mum.

Mrs Bunda: I know, but never mind, you are now a free person. See to your friends in case they get bored [*she moves into her kitchen*].

Busani: [*joins her friends who are having drinks*]: Are you enjoying yourselves, guys?

Nomsa: [*hugging Busani*]: It is so sweet to see you out of that awful yellow prison garb.

Busani: It was awful. The clothing crawled with lice and the food was horrible. The stench was overwhelming and each time I breathed, I just thought of the Covid-19 virus in the packed cells. It is a terrible place and I would not wish for anyone to spend a minute in there.

Tom: [*to Busani*]: Nice to see you again, girl!

Busani: [*she hugs Tom*]: I missed you so much guys [*they disengage from the embrace*].

Tom: [*to Jimmy*]: Since you are leaving in a hurry, we will talk over the phone about other matters. For now, enjoy yourself.

Jimmy: No problem my friend, we will be in touch.

Tom: So where are you going from here?

Jimmy: The less you know, the better. You may be forced by the police to reveal our whereabouts.

Tom: You are quite right [*hugs Jimmy*]: We will all miss you though.

Jimmy: Given what is happening, I would not be surprised if all of you grow wings soon.

Tom: I can see that coming. Every Tom will want a piece of our ill-gotten loot. The whole process will be repeated if one of us is arrested. I will check tonight if my passport still has valid visas.

Jimmy: In Harare, people don't sleep scheming ways to cream off others. Let me see to my future mother- in- law [*he goes into the kitchen*].

Busani: I think Tom is right guys; it is time for all of us to scamper.

Nomsa: Time to celebrate now! We will be leaving shortly for the airport. I will bring others around for a toast to your great escape.

Busani: Girl, I can't wait to go abroad, imagine being the lead story in the country's leading newspapers, let alone being the subject matter of discussion on other worldwide media platforms.

Nomsa: You will have the last laugh, my dear [*they embrace*].

Busani: I hope so, my dear. Did you get our Covid-19 tests results? Without those; we won't be able to fly out.

Nomsa: [*laughs*]: Oh, I nearly forgot [*she dips her hand into her handbag and brings out papers*]: It is all here, my friend, all sorted by the underworld, but legit.

Busani: [*smiles*]: Thank you very much, people have landed in trouble with forged tests results [*they hug*].

[*Exit all*].

Scene V

Opens at the Robert Gabriel Mugabe International Airport where Busani and Jimmy have just checked in for a flight to South Africa. Before going into the departure lounge, they engage with their families and close friends in farewell conversations.

Busani: [*approaches her mum and hugs her*]: All is in order mum.

Mrs Bunda: So, you can fly without any problems then?

Busani: Yes, the officials said everything is in order. Since my name is listed in the USA database as still having a valid visa to the USA, Nomsa caused my new passport to be stamped accordingly. She knows Harare people.

Mrs Bunda: Wonderful

Mrs Bunda: God is with you, my daughter. Make sure, you do not forget what I said about looking after Jimmy. We brought you up in a Christian family and taught you to be an upright person. Never forget your upbringing wherever you are...

Busani: [*interrupts her mum*]: Please mum, you have lectured me on those virtues on numerous occasions. There is no need to embarrass me here with another lecture.

Mrs Bunda: [*wiping a tear*]: Go well my daughter, look after yourself and Jimmy. Don't worry about us here, we will be okay.

Busani: [*also wiping tears*]: Okay, mum [*she hugs her mum*].

Mrs Bunda: I know God will look after you out there [*she looks heavenwards, then disengages from the hug and moves towards Jimmy*].

125

Jimmy: [*to Mrs Bunda*]: We will talk to you soon mum. Don't worry, I will look after Busani. As soon as we are settled, we will invite you and my mum for a visit.

Mrs Bunda: Thank you my son for taking this decision at the eleventh hour to leave everything and go with my daughter into the wilderness.

Jimmy: [*smiles*]: It is not into the wilderness mum; it's a better place than this country. My people will pay the bride price within 24 hours so that I am lawfully married to Busani.

Mrs Moyo: [*to Jimmy*]: Look after Busani, my son. We often hear of young men abandoning their wives in the diaspora. Don't embarrass us by adopting uncultured behaviour.

Jimmy: [*to his mum*]: That won't happen mum, I swear.

Mrs Moyo: [*holds Busani's hands*]: You are such an angel, beautiful and well brought up person. Before you even get to the States, Jimmy's relatives will have paid the bride price. By end of day tomorrow, you will be Mrs Moyo, my daughter [*she smiles*].

Busani: [*smiles*]: Thank you, mum.

Mrs Moyo: [*to Busani*]: If Jimmy becomes a problem, just give me a ring and I will sort him out.

Busani: [*smiles*]: I will mum.

Jimmy: [*to Busani*]: I think it is time for us to go for you never know who is at this airport.

Tom: [*hugs Jimmy*]: My friend, we will hook up in the First World very soon.

Jimmy: [*to Tom*]: You are quite right. We made a lot of money and the whole country wants a cut. Unfortunately, that is not going to happen.

Tom: Go well my friend [*he disengages himself from the hug*].

Busani: [*addresses the small gathering*]: Thank you, guys, for seeing us off, Jimmy and I need to go in now and board our flight. The sooner we leave this public place, the better [*they all hug, Jimmy and Busani head for the departure lounge).*

[*Exit all*].

Scene VI

Opens at Mr and Mrs Rengwe's house and present in the lounge are the Rengwes, the interpreter and his wife, Rose.

Mr Rengwe: [*to the interpreter*]: I heard the good news from your wife, my son.

Interpreter: [*smiles*]: We are very excited about the house we bought, Sir.

Mrs Rengwe: Thank you my son. My daughter can now bring up my grandchildren in a place she calls her own.

Rose: Mum, I am sick and tired of our landlady complaining about my supposed children's bad behaviour. Hardly a day passes without her threatening to throw us out.

Mrs Rengwe: [*scornfully*]: As a barren woman; she does not understand how difficult it is to bring up children.

Rose: She was not happy when I told her that we are moving from her house tomorrow. She did not like at all the one day notice I gave her.

Mrs Rengwe: It is difficult these days to get new and reliable tenants quickly. It serves her right though.

Interpreter: Her dismay is understandable as we are the only tenants who paid her on time and in US dollars.

Mr Rengwe: [*to the interpreter*]: I understand you bought the house on a cash basis. How did you manage that, my son?

Mrs Rengwe: It is quite a feat to do that. Normally, people buy houses over years through mortgages.

Interpreter: [*smiles*]: I have a small business which I have been running fruitfully for some time, Sir.

Mr Rengwe: Relying on your salary especially as a civil servant in this country will get you nowhere. Well done my son, we are very proud of you.

Rose: My husband works very hard [*she smiles*].

Mrs Rengwe: [*to her husband*]: Your daughter has just told me that they are having a house-warming party this very weekend. We are not waiting to be invited. We will be there before dawn! [*she smiles*].

Rengwe: That is good. It will be a good occasion to herald our daughter' success.

Mrs Rengwe: [*smiles*]. That will wipe the smugness off those who looked down upon my hard working and enterprising son-in-law.

Mr Rengwe: My wife, make sure you invite those who thought less of this young couple.

Rose: Mum, let me go into the kitchen and prepare the special meal with the grocery we brought you [*exit*].

Mrs Rengwe: Thank you very much my son for the big grocery. Times are really tough, and we really appreciate your support.

Interpreter: [*to Mrs Rengwe*]: Mum, my business is thriving and just today, I roped in a new partner which will result in more money coming in. There will be bigger groceries coming your way.

Mrs Rengwe: [*clasps her hands*]: Thank you, my son. Let me go and help your wife to cook [*exit*].

Interpreter: [*to Mr Rengwe*]: If you are not busy, Sir, can we go and have some cold ones at your local bottle store.

Mr Rengwe: [*smiles*]: That is a good idea. Let us go and drink to your success my son. All we hear about young people these days are their acts of thievery. I will tell my friends of your successful enterprise, my good son. Your ancestral spirits are with you and may they never forsake you. Well done indeed!

[*Exit both*].

ACT VII

Scene I

Opens with Mr Dehwa emerging from the arrivals section of the Robert Gabriel Mugabe International Airport, Harare and he sees Jimmy and Busani.

Dehwa: [*soliloquising*]: Ah! What is happening here? John sent me a message that Busani had been granted bail and but that her passport has been taken away. But here, it seems she is leaving the country [*following Busani and Jimmy, he rings John using his mobile*].

John: [*answers the call on his mobile*]: Mr Dehwa, are you back in the country, Sir?

Dehwa: Yes. Listen, I am just behind Busani who is heading into the airport's departure lounge.

John: [*feigns shock*]: What!

Dehwa: I thought you said Busani's was ordered not to leave the country?

John: [*feigning alarm*]: She has to be stopped, Sir! Please inform the airport security. I will speedily be there, and I am also informing the investigating officer right away.

Dehwa: Good. We need to act very, very fast [*he cuts the call and rushes to the departure desk, a move observed by Tom*].

131

Tom: Oh, my God! That is Mr Dehwa. He has seen Busani and Jimmy heading towards the departure lounge and is now following them.

Mrs Bunda: [*anxiously*]: Who is he?

Tom: He is one of the executives at our bank. He had travelled to South Africa in order to facilitate intensive, corrupt free investigations into the bank frauds.

Nomsa: Could he have heard while he was in South Africa that Busani's passport has been surrendered to the clerk of court?

Tom: Given these instant messages like WhatsApp, he might know.

Mrs Moyo: [*raises her hands heavenwards*]: Lord, please have mercy on Busani!

Mrs Bunda: [*also raises her hands to the heavens*]: Oh Lord, have pity on us! Lord, you cannot embarrass us at this last hurdle...

Tom: [*dejectedly*]: The game is up: the public address system is asking Busani and Jimmy not to board but to go back to the departure desk.

Nomsa: Oh, No!

Mrs Bunda: Why is it always us who are on the receiving end... [*she collapses*].

Mrs Moyo: [*to Tom*]: I am hard of hearing; did you say Jimmy's name was also called out?

Tom: Yes.

Mrs Moyo: [*to Tom*]: But is it not Busani who has a matter to settle with the court?

Tom: [*to Mrs Moyo*]: I am not sure, Mrs Moyo. However, a lot of money went missing at the bank and a number of bank tellers are suspected of having stolen it.

Mrs Moyo: [*moves away and soliloquises*]: Falling in love with Busani, that clever for nothing girl was Jimmy's Achilles heel. He started stealing to impress her with flashy cars, dining in those upmarket restaurants. I begged him to stop stealing from his employer, but he vehemently denied he was stealing.

His father, obviously, the recipient of part of the loot, defended his son, saying Jimmy had been promoted at the bank. Well, this is the end. I suppose the police will grab all those luxury intercountry buses [*she spits in contempt*].

[*Exit all*].

Scene II

Opens at the departure desk where Busani, Jimmy, Mr Dehwa, airport personnel and police officers are engaged in a conversation.

Departure Desk Attendant: [*to Busani*]: The reason we called you, madam, is because, this gentleman [*he points to Mr Dehwa*], told us you stole money from your workplace. He reported to us that you were granted bail today on condition that you surrender your passport and reside at your home address until the matter is finalised.

In short madam, you are not supposed to travel outside the country nor should you be in possession of a passport in your name. Is that the position?

Nomsa: [*trembles*]: Ah! Ah! [*she collapses*].

Sergeant: [*checks Busani*]: She is fine, there is no need to call an ambulance. She is just shell shocked.

Constable: The ambulance service is better off attending to deserving people and certainly not fraudsters.

Sergeant: Constable, help me to sit her up on the bench and make sure you keep an eagle eye on her.

Constable: To thwart any thoughts of gaining freedom ever again, I will handcuff her till the relevant police officer arrives [*he handcuffs Busani*].

Dehwa: [*turning to Jimmy*]: So, you were leaving with her?

Jimmy: [*angrily*]: I suppose you got your revenge for being spurned by her, you miserable, bald, shameless, married fat old man. I am going to smash you! [*he charges towards Mr Dehwa*].

Sergeant: [*grabs Jimmy*]: Hey! My friend, you have quite a nerve, to launch an assault upon the person of another before the very eyes of the law.

Jimmy: [*shouts*]: He is just being vindictive! He knows no more than a monkey what happened at the bank and yet, here he is, peddling lies. I am going to ... [*he lunges at Dehwa*].

Sergeant: [*stands between the fuming Jimmy and Dehwa*]: This is my last warning to you, young man. You are going to miss your flight if you persist in being a nuisance at this airport. Do you understand?

Jimmy: I am sorry officer.

Dehwa: [*shaken by Jimmy's charge*]: Officer, this guy also stole money from the bank. He was going to be arrested today. Fortunately for him, he did not turn up at the court where the police officer was lying in wait.

Jimmy: That is a lie. I have a plane to catch [*he hastily starts moving towards the departure lounge*].

Sergeant: [*shouts after Jimmy*]: Young man! I demand that you come back here now! We need to get to the bottom of the allegation levelled against you before you fly away!

Dehwa: [*shouts*]: Arrest him, officer, he is a fraudster! [*the sergeant rushes and grapples with Jimmy and during the fracas, bundles of US dollars spill out of Jimmy's bag*].

Sergeant: [*surprised*]: Ah! My friend, where did you get this large sum of money from?

Jimmy: [*defiantly*]: It is mine!

Departure Help Desk Attendant: [*having checked on his computer*]: From our records, you did not declare this large sum which by my mere sight, is well over the maximum allowed by law to be taken out of the country.

Dehwa: [*shrilly shouts*]: It is the bank's money!

Constable: [*sternly*]: Mr Dehwa, please calm down. There is no need to get excited.

Dehwa: [*uses his mobile phone to ring John*]: John, can you speak to this police constable in relation to Jimmy and your investigations [*he hands his phone to the constable*].

John: [*on his mobile phone*]: Hi, constable, I am the Barstan chief security officer and I would like to inform you that Jimmy Moyo must be stopped from leaving the country. There is a warrant for his arrest for theft of hundreds of US dollars. I will be with you very soon with the investigating officer.

Constable: [*on the phone*]: Thank you for the information. We will curtail his movement and you will find him here [*he hands the mobile phone back to Dehwa*].

Sergeant: [*violently pulls Jimmy by his belt to the desk*]: Constable, may you please count the money this gentleman intended to take out of the country.

Constable: [*receives Jimmy's satchel from the sergeant*]: Right away, sergeant! While you were engaged in that skirmish with the gentleman, I managed to speak to the bank security officer. He indicated to me that he is rushing to this airport in the company of the investigating officer to arrest this very gentleman [*he points a finger at Jimmy*] for fraud.

Jimmy: Oh, my God! [*he collapses*].

[*Exit all*].

Scene III

A distance away, Busani's relatives and friends watch the events unfolding at the airport departure desk.

Mrs Bunda: My sight is not that good. What is happening over there?

Tom: Busani and Jimmy have been handcuffed

Mrs Bunda: [*paces up and down*]: Oh, Holy Christ! Oh, Great Heavens, have mercy!

Mrs Moyo: [*shouts at Mrs Bunda*]: My poor love smitten son stole to impress a Harare slay queen. I told him to stay away from a yellow bone but he did not. What did my son really see in that stupid thief?

Mrs Bunda: [*shouting and wagging a finger at Mrs Moyo*]: So, my daughter is now a slay queen and a thief? If that was so, we would expect those luxury buses to be in Busani names, but they are in your husband's name! That long-time pauper husband of yours became a success story overnight! Tell him, the police are hard on his heels! [*she spits*].

Mrs Moyo: [*shaken, she moves away and soliloquises*]: So, the community has known all along about the acquisition of those luxury coaches. This is the end of us then. The media will be here soon, it is best I disappear and leave this foulmouthed woman to entertain them [*exit*].

Nomsa: [*to Mrs Bunda who has started sobbing*]: Please mum stop crying. We don't know what is really happening over there.

Tom: [*drawing Nomsa aside*]: Nomsa, even a fool can tell that it is all over. The wheels, my dear, have come off and those two love birds [*points at Busani and Jimmy*] are bound for the maximum-security prison. If we don't do something quickly, we will certainly dine with them very soon.

Nomsa: [*anxiously*]: So, what do we do?

Tom: We are leaving the country now; I saw this coming and made plans. We are going to Kariba now.

Nomsa: Kariba?

Tom: I planned with my cousins who are fishermen in Kariba. Let's go [*he pulls her by her hand*].

Nomsa: [*she struggles to go to Mrs Bunda*]: Let me, at least say goodbye to Mrs Bunda.

Tom: [*pulls her away*]: This is not the time to be seen consorting with the fallen [*both exit*].

Mrs Bunda: [*looks around and soliloquises*]: It seems no one is going to hang around here anymore. The vultures are gleefully recording this drama and soon, we will become breaking news on various social media platforms. Nonetheless, I will wait and see what happens to my daughter. I will also see to it that the police officers are fair by arresting all bank tellers including Nomsa and Tom. They are in this together and must go down together [*exit*].

Scene IV

The same day, late at night, John, the prosecutor, the magistrate and the interpreter are engaged in mobile phone conversations.

John: [*to the prosecutor*]: My friend, sorry for calling you at this late hour, but you have a big problem, a very big one.

Prosecutor: [*alarmed*]: What is it now?

John: Lady Luck ran out on Busani and the plan for her to leave the country has run aground.

Prosecutor: What happened?

John: The police have not only arrested her for breaching her bail conditions, but they are going to bring her to your court for her to explain herself.

Prosecutor: [*the mobile phone falls from his hand*]: Oh, my God! [*he picks up his mobile phone*].

John: The media frenzy regarding this saga is very astonishing. It is viral, it is like a veld fire, my friend. I am a lay man at law, but I think man, you have a problem, a very big one.

Prosecutor: Yes, it's a mammoth problem. Ordinarily, justice will demand that she be remanded in custody for breach of her bail conditions is she fails to give a satisfactory account. However, our court which facilitated her flight will be called upon to deal with her flagrant disregard for the bail conditions. It will be very onerous for me to stand up in court and demand that she be remanded in custody well knowing that I took part in facilitating her flight in return for a bribe.

John: It is not only your problem. How about His Worship?

Prosecutor: I equally doubt His Worship would remand her in custody knowing fully well that she will talk about the whole deal. Equally, if she is released, questions will be raised and we, without doubt whatsoever, will be called to account by the justice system. I can imagine the media frenzy over this catastrophe. Can you imagine the headlines?

John: Headlines are the least of your problems my friend. The investigating officer has been ordered by his bosses to arrest all known suspects. This includes Nomsa and Tom whom you have already met. Jimmy has already been arrested at the airport for fraud and to compound his woes, he was found with bundles of money which he can't account for.

Prosecutor: Jimmy's case is like a sparrow worrying a hawk to me.

John. I wouldn't hasten to say that my friend. I went to the holding cells at the police station and had a private chat with the lovers who demanded that I should tell you to pull strings. They are demanding that you cause their release forthwith, or they will squeal.

Prosecutor: Ok, I will ring you shortly. Let me see what I can do.

John: Okay, good luck [*exit*].

Prosecutor: [*soliloquises*]: My ancestors have deserted me in my hour of greatest need. What can I do now? Let me inform His Worship about this great tragedy and maybe he has a trick up his sleeve [*he picks his phone and rings him*].

Magistrate: [*answers the prosecutor's call*]: My friend, this is a very late call. Is everything okay?

Prosecutor: Had it not been for this breaking news, I would not have rung you, my friend. We are on the brink of a great calamity.

Magistrate: [*rises from the bed he is sharing with his wife who is asleep*]: Hold on [*he moves into the lounge and talks in a hushed tone*]. What is it?

Prosecutor: Busani has been arrested at the airport contrary to the bail conditions you set. She is in police custody now and as per procedure; she will be brought to your court to explain her conduct. I understand the boyfriend has also been arrested. They want strings pulled. They said anything short of their immediate release will result in them spilling the beans.

Magistrate: [*defensively*]: But I did not receive any money personally. It is you whom they dealt with.

Prosecutor: Your Worship, you know from previous court cases that that line of defence won't hold water.

Magistrate: So, what do we do? We can't just release her again.

Prosecutor: Now you are thinking. I am not waiting for them to come to court.

Magistrate: What do you mean?

Prosecutor: Are you going to wait for the sensational trial of the year. Picture this: you, the magistrate, and I, the prosecutor and the interpreter hauled before the courts for corruption. How about throwing in whoever processed that passport and to spice it up, haul in also the celebrated courier?

Magistrate: I see what you mean. It will be the trial of the century. Notwithstanding that the maximum-security prison is bursting at the seams, they will easily find room for us. So, what do you propose we do?

Prosecutor: I am sorry I can't divulge my plans to you [*he switches off his phone and exits*].

Magistrate: Hallo! Hallo! [*soliloquises*]: He has hung up on me! This is what Martha warned me about. What am I going to do now? I need at least to warn the interpreter [*he uses his phone to ring the interpreter*].

Interpreter: [*answers his phone with a slur and in the background, loud Zimdancehall music can be heard*]. His Worship, how are you?

Magistrate: You seem to be having a good time.

Interpreter: Why not in this land of milk and honey? I am drinking fine waters, singing along to Soul Jah Love's *Pamamonya Ipapo* song. If you haven't heard the song, Soul Jah Love is saying notwithstanding the odds, he is standing among the giants.

Magistrate: Well, my friend, that was then.

Interpreter: How is that? How can it be? I am a proud owner of a brandy new house. I am the only interpreter in a housing scheme of moneyed people. I will be living among giants from tomorrow, Your Worship…

Magistrate: [*he interrupts the interpreter*]: Hold on, my friend. That deal has blown in our faces. Our friends have been arrested at the airport upon trying to flee the country.

Interpreter: What has that to do with me?

Magistrate: When you get sober, you will appreciate the implications of their arrest [*he switches off his phone and exits*].

Interpreter: [*soliloquises*]: Foolish magistrate! Is it me who granted the fraudster bail? What arrant nonsense! [*he takes a swig at his beer, burps and exits*].

Scene V

Opens the next day with the magistrate, the prosecutor and the interpreter soliloquising.

Enter the magistrate.

Magistrate: [*soliloquises*]: This is the worst day of my life. I am not waiting for my trial or else I will die in prison. It is a shame that I have to leave the country without my dear wife and children. My wife did warn me though, but anyway, that is water under the bridge. They will join me as soon as I am settled across the border.

To allay any suspicion that I have bolted, I have left my pickup truck at home. In making haste, my chances of surreptitiously skipping the country will be enhanced through hitch hiking. If there is a public bulletin pertaining to my pursuit by the police, I will stick out as a sore thumb on public transport. Let me double check that I have my passport, educational certificates, money and leave for Botswana [*exit*].

Enter the prosecutor.

Prosecutor: [*soliloquises*]: Only a fool will wait for the inevitable onslaught from the courts. If I tarry here, I will soon become a long-time resident at the maximum-security prison. It may even be a short sojourn, given the presence of those highly aggrieved accused persons. Strangely, every accused person believes it is the prosecutor's fault that there are in prison. Well, they won't be laying their dirty hands on me. Even the COVID-19 virus will not find me there.

Let me make haste for the Masvingo highway and catch private transport to Beitbridge and then into South Africa but not through the border. Only a fool who is on the run will travel on public transport, so I will hitch hike [*he pauses*]: Let me check my essentials. Added to my loot of US$300 000 is my meagre savings of US$300. Setting out with US$300 300 is by all standards not bad at all for a young man with no family ties. My educational certificates and my passport are all here. So, here is to plan B [*exit*].

Enter the interpreter at his newly purchased house.

Interpreter: [*soliloquises*]: What a disgrace. In my sound and sober senses, I now understand fully what His Worship meant last night. I saw Busani and Jimmy being brought to court two hours ago. The way Jimmy looked at me made me tremble. His face said it all and I had to leave the court building. Worryingly, His Worship and the prosecutor were conspicuously absent at the court today. I have tried on numerous times to ring their mobile phones but they are all unreachable. I suspect they have made friends with the wind and here I am, in this ill-gotten house.

Our deal will become public soon. Just yesterday, my father-in-law was lauding me as the epitome of an honest businessman. Businessman, my foot! What a disgrace to my family and in-laws. The house will most likely be confiscated by the court as proceeds of crime. Only a fool will wait to be manacled. I have to make friends with the wind... [*his mobile rings and he answers*]: Hello Mike...

Mike: [*on his phone*]: Where are you, my friend?

Interpreter: What's up Mike?

Mike: My friend, a huge number of police officers have searched every nook of this building, but they could not find you. They have now split up into two forces; one group has sped to your-in-laws and another to your lodgings hoping to lay their hands on you.

Interpreter: Why are they after me?

Mike: I understand it concerns a case involving a bank teller who appeared in your court recently. She and her boyfriend called Jimmy, currently confined at the courts have been singing. The enormity of what they said caused them to be taken back to the police station for further investigations before the court hears her explanation for breaching her bail conditions. They said you were the middleman who arranged the … [*the interpreter cuts the call*]: Hello, hello…[*exit*].

Interpreter [*soliloquises*]: This is it then. I will execute Plan B [*exit*].

Scene VI

Opens at a state television broadcasting centre a day later with the broadcaster Rovapasi Zvaramba interrupting a running programme.

Rovapasi Zvaramba: Good afternoon. We apologise for interrupting this programme, but we have some breaking news from the Harare's Rotten Row magistrates court where there has been some sensational news. There has been a new twist in the alleged multi-million US dollar fraud perpetrated against Barstan bank.

Busani Bunda who has lately been in the news for a massive fraud has appeared in court moments ago to explain why she breached her bail conditions. Parts of the bail conditions were that she should reside at her home till the matter is finalised and also to surrender her passport. She was arrested two days ago while trying to flee the country. In her explanation, she told the court that a magistrate, a prosecutor and an interpreter working collaboratively and corruptly, facilitated her flight in return for hundreds of US Dollars. For the breach, she has been remanded in custody and the court has estreated her bail. Her boyfriend, Jimmy Moyo, who also worked at the bank was arrested at the airport for similar offences and appeared in court and was denied bail as he is said to be a flight risk.

A police spokeswoman has given out that they are in hot pursuit of some bank tellers whom they want to question in connection with the massive significant loss suffered by the bank. This is the end of the breaking news and we hope you will enjoy the rest of your viewing, have a good day [*exit*].

Scene VII

Opens a day later at the Harare Central Police Station where a police spokeswoman is giving a press conference.

Police Spokeswoman: Ladies and gentlemen of the press, I welcome you all. I am going to give you an update on the on-going Barstan fraud case which has drawn immense national and international interest. The force is working flat out to bring the crooks to book.

You are aware that Busani Bunda is back in remand prison where justice demands she must be. Also, her boyfriend, Jimmy Moyo is also in remand prison, awaiting trial. You are also aware that Busani told the court that her escape involved the nefarious activities of court officials.

Sadly, ladies and gentlemen, we have been denied justice, firstly by the interpreter who acted as the intermediary in the deal. The interpreter has been found hanging in his newly bought house which we strongly believe was funded from the ill-gotten money. We are not treating his death as suspicious.

Further, justice has been thwarted, members of the press. A dismembered human body has been identified positively as being that of the prosecutor who corruptly released Busani. The body was fished out of the Limpopo River and we believe the deceased was attacked by crocodiles while attempting to cross into South Africa illegally. Although the information we received suggests that he had up to US$300 000 when he took flight, only US$5 was recovered from his body. We believe the prosecutor's larger loot which was on his body could have been consumed in the melee by crocodiles.

However, all is not lost as an employee from the Registrar General's office who is alleged to have facilitated the processing of a passport to enable Busani Bunda to leave the country has been nabbed and is helping us with our investigations.

In widening our net, our meticulous investigations revealed other actors who were involved in the massive bank fraud. Topping the list were Mr Tom Kanye and Miss Nomsa Kacheche. Our diligent investigations have led to the recovery on the shores of Lake Kariba, the latest Toyota Prado SUV registered in Tom's grandfather, a man who has been living abject poverty in his rural home for ages. We were reliably informed that the two accused persons crossed illegally by night into Zambia on a boat. The fishermen who helped them to escape justice are currently in custody and will face the full wrath of the law.

We quickly liaised with our counterparts in Zambia and Interpol to locate and arrest the duo. Our equally relentless counterparts have informed us that today, they commanded a UK bound plane which was already airborne to return to Lusaka Airport whereupon they seized Tom and Nomsa. We have despatched our colleagues to bring them back home and face justice.

Leaving no stone unturned, I would like to inform you ladies and gentlemen of the press that the Covid-19 tests results that were tendered at the airport by Busani and Jimmy have turned to be forgeries. I am very happy to inform you that the originators of those documents have been arrested and are assisting us with our investigations.

We have also found details of other persons who obtained false, bogus Covid-19 virus test results from these bogus people. We are in no doubt that these fraudsters have been dishing out false negative Covid-19 test results to hundreds of people to enable them to travel within and outside Zimbabwe. We therefore have names and addresses of people who obtained false negative Covid-19 test results to travel and undoubtedly, we will be knocking at people's addresses.

Further, ladies and gentlemen, our robust investigations have revealed that the magistrate who allegedly corruptly granted bail to Busani was whipped at a village court for crossing the border illegally into Botswana. We have swiftly dispatched our officers to bring him to Harare for him to answer the allegations of corruption.

It is evident to you and the whole country that the police force is working day and night and all year round to deal with crime. However, given the on-going investigations, I am unable to answer your questions. That is all I have for you now and thank you for coming.

The End

Kennedy Mupomba was born in the then Rhodesia in 1969. Since the publication of his short stories in *Meet the Family* in the United Kingdom, he has also published *Of Fools and Justice*. Kennedy worked as a public prosecutor in the Zimbabwe's Ministry of Justice, Legal and Parliamentary Affairs. He is working as a social worker in the United Kingdom and holds bachelor degrees in Applied Community Studies, Law and masters degrees in Social Policy and Social Work.

Of Fools
and
Justice

Kennedy Mupomba

Faced with an encounter with justice, most of us will try to enhance our standing by all means. Some may engage lawyers, prophets, witch doctors and some may bribe court offcials to evade the proper course of justice. In this play, two acused persons engaged a lawyer and a witch doctor but unknown to the other accused person, the other, to bolster his precaruos position engaged a prophet resulting in a disaster for both of them.